Cover Image by Derrick Peynado (DP Photo)
Edited By Kalita Cox

ISBN 978-0-9741914-8-5
Printed In U.S.A

Published by Mylk n Honee Publishing LLC.
www.becomingmonsta.com

I0593585

DEDICATIONS

To my team of life managers:
Kiwan, Tia, Ghana, D, Shawn and Ed...
Thank you for helping me keep the goal realistic and
attainable. This is as much your project as it is mine.

To DP,
Thank you for always executing my vision better than I
could have imagined it.

To Tracy, Mister Smith, E. Cruz, Robyn, Ty,
Rashidah, Mark and Chayce,
My characters have been brought to life because you
made it so. Thank you.

MONSTA°

[mon-stuh]

noun

1. A submissive who knows the power in kneeling and wields it to her benefit.

2. A woman who embraces her sexual prowess and is not afraid to snatch souls

CHAPTER 1
The Awakening

I remember the belt that cracked across my ass, plunging me into this lifestyle. I was face down, ass up in his bed, blindfolded and my hands tied behind my back with the necktie he wore to work that day. I didn't know what to expect. I had been begging him for a while to take me down the "Rabbit Hole" as he called it, yet he was hesitant. Likely because he knew more than I did about what I was asking for. I guess it was just the fact that I've always felt this urge to be dominated - to surrender my power to another person and let them control my every move that had me anxious to find out how deep that hole could go.

We had been together for about a year at this point. I knew he was into kinky shit, but in all that time, he was still holding back from me the full extent of it all. He knew my curiosity had been piquing ever since he told me he could be very crafty with ordinary household objects like spatulas, mason jars and cherry stems. The fact that it had been a while since we became a couple and he had yet to introduce me to what I would later discover was BDSM had me disheartened. I felt like I had been good to him. Everything about me exuded submission so what was his hang up? Considering that's how I felt, I never saw it coming. That night... the paradigm shifted.

He called my phone at about 3:30 that afternoon and told me to come through. I didn't have to work the next day, so I figured, why not. I was just closing out my workday when his call was received. It always thrilled me to see the pet name I gave him and a picture of us as his photo ID pop up on my screen. I called him "Smooch" so every time he'd call, I'd hear kissing noises and got happy. I told him I would be there after I picked up something for dinner and showered. I did a large majority of the cooking as he was mostly accustomed to ordering out before I came into his life, so it was simply second nature to grab what ingredients I needed.

It was about 6 pm when I got there. We gave each other a kiss and exchanged pleasantries. He seemed distant but he was never the one to show emotion, so I just brushed it off as him having a long day. As I prepared dinner, he reclined in his man-chair and turned to a sports channel. He was a partner in the city's only Black-owned law firm and his days were usually pretty stressful, so I always made a conscious effort to allow space for him to decompress. As the pots and pans started understanding their purposes, the scent of rosemary filled the air. I fancied myself a decent cook and made him lamb chops, asparagus, and wild rice to eat. As the sizzling and boiling created a harmonic flow, I quietly brought him a beer. He didn't look at me or make any sort of contact other than reaching his hand out to accept the beverage. I was beginning to think he was upset with me, but I know I couldn't have done anything wrong to receive the frigidness he displayed.

He was very quiet over supper - barely said a word. The only sound heard was the clanking of fork to plate. He didn't even allow himself to be heard chewing his food. He didn't put the fork down once which showed me that he at least liked the food I prepared, but his silence told me he was in deep thought. It wasn't anger or frustration that draped his face. It was as if he were calculating to himself or even reviewing evidence files in his mind. That's it. He brought work home with him, I thought. I immediately stopped internalizing what I was looking at and finished my meal. After my second glass of Riesling, I noticed him staring at me intensely - almost as if he was trying to pierce my soul with his glance.

"What?", I smiled. He said nothing but just kept staring and did so for at least 10 minutes. Air escaped my lungs with each meeting of our eyes. He was still clad in his work clothes which was odd, but I overlooked it and considered he just wanted to be dressed over dinner. His plate had nothing but bones remaining. He cleaned the corners of his mouth and fingertips with a napkin then rested his wrists on the table. His eyes stared a hole right through me like sunlight through a magnifying glass and a shaking leaf. No words left his lips -just intense staring. Nothing moved. He sat there looking like a picture. I couldn't even tell if he was still breathing or not. Worry began to set in again. Were we going to have a conversation about something? Did he find the new vibrator in my nightstand when he slept at my place the night before? What was going on?

The silence was broken by the legs of his chair dragging against the floor as he got up from his seat at the head of the table. He walked to me, gently taking my hand. I stood up, hand in his, feeling my anxiety turn into nervousness. I remember his dreads being pinned up. He had a lot of hair that he took much pride in keeping up with. I loved the way they fell next to his face when he had them down, but it made me swoon every time when he had them up. The god in him always showed itself when he had them up. I stood looking at the 6 foot 4, chocolate skinned god dead in his dark brown eyes and felt love. His light blue button-down shirt hugged his arms and torso perfectly. The shape he was in was immaculate – thick, chiseled, and solid. Samson himself could never. He looked me up and down briefly. I felt a knot swell up in my belly. He never looked at me that way before - like I was a quest to be conquered.

"Take your clothes off," he calmly commanded. The simple direction came roaring in like a tsunami washing away any doubt I previously had. For those to be the first words he spoke the entire evening shocked me, but I was far from upset. My honeywell jumped at the sound of his voice and with no delay, my skirt dropped to the floor. As I stepped out of it, I began unbuttoning my blouse, revealing the hunter green lace bra holding my breasts. He watched me the entire time. There was still no emotion in his face. The hairs on my arms began to raise from all the goosebumps that formed. Bra unhooked, matching panties trailing down my legs, I stood there naked before him. He stepped closer to me, kissed me softly then bit my bottom lip. His kiss was feathery against the sharpness of his teeth with my lip in between them. I winced but a soft moan couldn't help but slip out.

"Are you sure this is what you want," he asked. All sound other than his voice and my beating heart muted itself. My memories jolted back to the first time we met and how his smile drew me in. They zipped forward to the first time we made love; it was slow and sensual. The first sign of aggression flashed before my eyes and images of his hands around my neck filled my head as I listened to him continue speaking.

"Because once you go down this hole, there's no turning back." My excitement heightened as I immediately realized what he was speaking of. Eyes glazed over in enchantment; my gaze began to match his.

"So, are you ready?" he asked again. I nodded my head.

"Say it," he ordered. The authority in his voice made me melt. The confidence I felt build up the first time I told him I wanted to know what this life was like began to fill me again. I lifted my head with a pride that felt familiar to me.

"Yes. Ruin me." I requested with confidence. He smirked and traced his finger across my cheek gently. Leaning down toward my neck, I felt his kiss land on it, finding its way to my ear lobe. My forehead rested on his shoulder in relief, and I inhaled his scent. Everything about him was hypnotic. The breath in his nostril blew down my collarbone and he took a deep breath, exhaled, and whispered into my ear.

"Go get in my bed." He ordered.

I couldn't have run any faster up the stairs. The carpet became like velvet under my feet. The air I ran through was chilly enough to make my nipples harder than they already were. My excitement caused the hallway to become longer as if it knew of my impending doom and was trying to save me. When I entered the room, it looked different. He didn't rearrange any furniture or change the color scheme, but it wasn't the same room I previously walked into. Somehow, I associated it with both a death and re-birth. This was the room I was about to be introduced to a whole new world in. Every light was on. The comforter looked as if he pressed it before I got there. The sheets underneath was a brighter shade of red than I last remembered. There was a separate pillow-case at the edge of the bed that I noticed but bypassed as him simply forgetting to put it away with the rest of his laundry. A warmth lingered in the cotton scented air, filling my nose with tranquility. I climbed into the bed, allowing my skin to adjust to the coldness of the comforter. My body quickly warmed it up as I laid on my back dead in the center of the king-sized bed, covered in pillows. The anticipation was killing me. 'This is it!' I thought. I'm finally going to get what I've been pleading for. My flower blossomed just from the thought of what was getting ready to happen. I had fantasized about that very moment for so long – even rehearsed possible things I would say to him in the heat of passion. I had practiced telling him what positions I wanted it in, whether I wanted it fast or slow and even had my own collar picked out. The very little bit I did know, I learned from the internet and various movies. No one warned me prior to, that, that wasn't how any of it worked in real life.

I remember him taking his time coming upstairs. I tried to focus my ears on the hallway to see if I could hear his footsteps coming up the stairs so that when he came in, I could be in a sexy position for him. I heard nothing and was caught off guard when he finally came into the room, I eagerly sat up to receive him. All of my practice and preparation failed me. As I sat on my legs, poised, he leaned over, kissed my forehead, and told me to lay on my stomach. As I did, he recalled to me a memory of how I once expressed to him a few of my desires. The room turned completely dark as he cut each light out one by one. There was a breeze dancing on my skin coming from the window - a welcomed sensation against the warm, thick air circulating around the room. The down comforter kissed all over me. While I was laying there listening, I heard the sound of him untying his necktie and him pulling it from around his neck. I didn't give it a second thought until he took my hands and tied them behind my back with it. My heart started racing as he then took my feet and tied them at the ankles with another necktie. What the hell was about to happen? Mandisa, what did you just agree to? I asked myself. As nervous as I became, I felt my kitty start throbbing a lot harder than it already was. I was anxious for what was coming next. As I was least expecting it, in a bold move, he took the lone pillowcase and put it over my head just below my nose to blindfold me. Waves of excitement surged through my body. I had never experienced this. This was not shaping into anything I had formerly considered. My stomach felt like I was skydiving off the Grand Canyon.

As I lay there completely at his mercy, I hear his belt swoosh from around his waist then a sudden crack of it over my head. I jumped but remained still. I could feel the blood coursing through me. My pulse felt pronounced, especially in my most erogenous zones. The belt was slowly traced across the back of my legs. I could feel his eyes on me - staring at me, watching me like I was his canvas he was about to paint. He kept softly dragging the belt across the entire back of my body.

"You've been begging me to turn you since we've been together. I've tried to save you the entire time, but you just kept poking the sleeping beast. You just couldn't leave it be. Your curiosity is about to get you into a kind of trouble you can't get out of, Mandisa," he said in a stern tone. How bad could it be though?

WHAP!

10

My bound body curled up as I screamed from the heat of the belt that was just cracked across my ass. Grazing it lightly over my back, he came to the side of the bed where I was squirming to get into position, leaned over my ear, draped the belt across me and mildly chuckled.

"Get acquainted with that. Your safe word is Neruda. Welcome to your first night of training."

Face still covered by the pillowcase, I gasped as I heard his footsteps become distant. Where did he go? Why was he leaving me here in this state? What was his plan? Training? Was this going to be like bootcamp?! Safe word?! Ne-what?! Every relatable thought whizzed through my mind. I was slightly fearful yet immensely turned on in the same space. The sting my ass endured had begun to simmer down, and I was able to rest my body completely on the bed. My arms got a little uncomfortable from being tied up and my neck started to ache from laying my head on its side and being flat on the bed unable to move freely. Trying to relax, the pillowcase slipped from over my eyes, and I was able to look around into pitch black.

He left me by myself with my thoughts, tied up on his bed for a good 15-20 minutes. My mind was racing just as fast as my heart was. I recalled him asking if I was sure I wanted this. Being tied up in such an uncomfortable way almost had me second guessing my decision. It was the idea of being helpless that kept me intrigued. Was this a thing? Was I the only one that found pleasure in feeling destitute? Why would anyone want to feel this way? There had to be something wrong with me because...I loved it! So much so that I stayed lost in my thoughts until I heard his footsteps again. They were heavy this time, striking a slight fear in me once again. He came into the room at a steady pace, and I could smell his cologne again. I gently shook my head and bit my bottom lip, inhaling deeply. He always smelled so good. I lost my breath.

When he came back to me, he noticed that the pillowcase had slightly uncovered my face. Before putting it back over my head, he licked my jawline and said there are rules that if I am to be his submissive, I must follow. Hearing this caused my interest to be aroused. I never had to follow a man's rules before as I was always the one setting them. He had my full attention. As he spoke,

11

he untied my hands and allowed me to sit up. I sat on my still-bound legs and rubbed my wrists. Head bowed and eyes closed, I paid close attention to the direction his voice was coming from. His first rule is that I had to address him as either Daddy, Sir or Master; which one didn't matter to him. I liked Daddy.

Once he laid out his first rule, he asked if the terms were acceptable. I was so caught up in the moment, that I simply responded "Yes". My first mistake as his sub. He grabbed me by my neck, pushing my head down to the bed so that my ass was high in the air. He cracked his belt smooth across my ass for the second time.

"I see you don't listen. Yes...what?"

I cried out "Yes Daddy!" to which he praised a mellow, "Good girl..." I began to squirm under his strong grip. It felt like sparks started from my ass and tidal waved through my entire body as if I were a hookah coal someone just lit.

Rule number two: I was to keep a journal. In it, I was to write all my wants, needs, desires, fantasies, and feelings. If he made me happy, I was to write about it. If he made me angry, I was to write about it. Rubbing my body with one hand while still pinning me down at the neck with the other, he asked if the terms were acceptable. Still writhing in bliss, and unable to open my legs, I moaned and responded.

"Yes, Daddy."

His third rule was the most important he said. He finally untied my feet and sat me up so that I was kneeling on the bed. He cut one of the lights on so that we could see each other. When he came back to me, he raised the pillowcase, lifted my head by my chin with his curled index finger and said he needed me to look at him when he laid his next rule out because he needed to stress its imperativeness. In this rule, he reiterated my safe word. He defined what it was and in what instances I should use it. Once I acknowledged that I understood, he draped the pillowcase back over my head loosely and we practiced. The first exercise involved him biting me until I screamed my safe word to gauge my pain tolerance. He asked me if I was able to move onto the second exercise. When I said that I could, he pinched my nipples with increasing pressure until I said my safe word. Once he soothed the pain, he praised me for doing such a good job and said we had one final bit of practice, if I could handle it, then positioned my head back down to the bed when I agreed.

He began spanking me at the level he first struck me and went higher in intensity each time. With each slap I jumped, winced, and even grunted but I never uttered my safe word. After a few minutes, he paused and told me to hold my position before backing away to sit down. While face down, ass up, my body involuntarily gyrated as moans cliff jumped out of my gut. The perfectly straight sheets became wrinkled in my clenched fists. Waves of electricity oceaned back and forth through my flesh. I had no idea what was happening to me. The pain I had just endured felt comforting to me like a cozy blanket wrapped around me. I called to my love, but he refused to answer. He sat in what now looked like a throne to me and watched me beg for him, belt still in hand. When he finally came back to me, my body seemed able to tolerate more pain as he resumed the spanking. He began at the level he ended the first round with, but with his hand this time and I took it like a champ. I didn't even flinch. This must have pleased him because I could sense the approval in the way he spoke to me. He increased the intensity with every blow, spacing the hits out to allow my skin to recover. He rubbed each spot he hit immediately after each time. He kept saying things like "good girl" and "look at you" which made me crave more. The painful sensation began to creep up again. The harder the blow the louder the grunt. My body rolled all over the bed and if I fell flat, he would spank me again.

"Stay where I put you!" he exclaimed. Forcing myself back into position, I could feel my juices seeping out. With each slap across my ass, I came closer to the brink of insanity. Just as I was about to scream my safe word, he took his hand and slowly slid it between my legs to feel how aroused I was. He leaned down and softly growled into my ear...

"Who said you could get wet? Clearly, you need more training"

I got wetter. I was on the verge of explosion. He kept rubbing my soft while I still had the pillowcase over my head. I felt myself about to cum, so I rushed to ask him for permission. He told me no, but it was too late. I had already begun to orgasm so hard. He reached all the way under me and felt it all. I could hear the grin on his face.

13

"It's ok. You couldn't help it. This is your first night as my submissive. You'll learn. I forgive all of your mistakes tonight," and went back to rubbing on my clit. The passion was overwhelming. This was a side of him I truly had mistaken. He had the perfect balance of aggression and calmness, speaking to me as if I was a new pet he was house breaking, all the while coaxing my pussy to cum again in the softest manner. After I came a second time, he leaned down into my ear.

"Isn't Daddy a generous Master?" he asked.

I was so high I could barely get "Yes Daddy" out. As he brought the session to a close, I was stuck in the clouds, my body limp and lifeless. When he realized I was spent, he yanked the pillowcase off my head, squeezed my face and laid out his final rule. It was that moment, upon hearing it, I knew I no longer belonged to myself, and I was ok with that. He made me cum several times that night and didn't even fuck me. It was all about breaking me in. I became cold and began shivering. He laid next to me, talking to me in soft, low tones, reassuring me that he was right there, which I later learned was called "aftercare". I was so gone. It felt like I sniffed an entire kilo of pure Columbian cocaine to the face. When I was stable, he kissed my cheek, said "you're welcome" and left out of the room to go back downstairs. I drifted slowly into peaceful sleep. My body felt so new. I had found everything I needed. Stars danced above my head the entire night. There I was, Mandisa Bloom: a newly dominated submissive and it hurt so good...

CHAPTER 2
Lead and She'll Follow

"Aziz, pass me the butter, please?" she asked me, unaware of what she was about to get herself into. Mandisa made a mean ass lamb chop and after the day I had, I practically swallowed the plate whole.

She had been begging me for months to make her my submissive. She had confided in me a while ago that she just has this innate need to be controlled and didn't know where it came from. If my memory served me correctly, a girlfriend of hers suggested she just might be a natural submissive and urged her to do some research on BDSM. During the conversation, I revealed to her that I'm a part of the lifestyle and identify as a Dominate. I don't think I've ever seen her eyes twinkle that hard after telling her that. Once the cat was out of the bag, she continuously pushed the issue. I was reluctant to show her my world because I always saw her as a good girl and this life could completely destroy her. But, after much poking and prodding, I decided to turn her.

I stayed silent during dinner on purpose. I wanted her to feel a slight tension to catch her off guard. She was on her second or third glass of wine. I just stared at her. There was a slight squint in my eyes as I contemplated all the ways I was going to demolish her. Her breasts sat nice and perfectly in the blouse she had on. Her caramel skin looked like it absorbed all the sunlight that day. Her hair was pulled up into a ponytail, so I was definitely getting a handful of that in a little while. Yea...she was ready. She looked at me confused. I'm sure she was wondering what the problem was. Good. That's exactly where I wanted her.

After I finished eating, I stood and walked over to her. I took her by the hand and pulled her to me. In my heart, I was still resisting turning her. She was just so innocent - such a good woman. She went to church - sang in the choir and all, but something in me just wanted to make her scream several Hallelujahs to the mountains with my belt. She looked at me with those loving eyes. What was I about to do to this woman? Would she even be able to take it? How would she look at me in the morning? Could she handle my burning desire to control everything around me, including her? I pulled myself together and looked her in her eyes. These were her last moments as the sweet, timid "Mandi" I knew.

"Take your clothes off," I told her. She moved with such haste. Her eagerness pleased me. I asked her was she sure this is

16

what she wanted. I told her if she falls down this rabbit hole, there was no turning back. She wouldn't want to come back. I asked again.

"So, are you ready?" I asked. She nodded her head.

"Say it," I ordered. I saw the last bit of righteousness leave her eyes. A seriousness and confidence rained down over her face.

"Yes. Ruin me" she replied. Her response shocked me slightly, but I didn't let it show in my face. Little did she know I was about to break every bit of confidence in her voice. I watched her thick thighs and plump ass switch all the way up the staircase. I wasn't quick to follow her, though. I let her wait - let the anticipation flood her mind and body. I sat down on my couch and continued watching sports highlights. My left arm was draped over the top of my couch, and I was stretched comfortably across it. In my mind, I knew Mandi was upstairs in my bed losing her shit. Why wouldn't she be, considering this was what she had been begging for. I drew her readiness out to the last possible minute before heading upstairs. I didn't want her to hear me coming so I quieted my footsteps purposely to startle her. When I finally stepped into the bedroom, she was laying on the bed, anxious to see what this life was all about. Seeing me walk in, she sat up zealously, thinking we were about to embrace each other.

"Nah. Lay on your stomach." I told her after kissing her on the forehead. There was a slight hesitation, but she did as I commanded. She once told me about a few fantasies she had - how she ached to live them out with me. I recalled them to her as I stood over her naked, waiting body. The savage started to rise up in me. Like a vampire, I was about to sink my teeth into her soul and turn her into my greatest masterpiece.

I began to untie my tie. I hadn't even taken the gators off my feet. If I was to turn her, it would be as a true boss. I bound her hands at the wrist with the tie. I heard a soft gasp come from her. Her legs were too free to move for me, so I pulled another necktie out of my drawer and tied those together too. Her breathing got heavier. I took it one step further and snatched the pillowcase I strategically left on the bed and loosely covered her face with it. I stood back to study her reaction. She softly gyrated on the bed and allowed soft moans to enter the air. The grin on my face told it all.

I unfastened my belt, took it off and popped it directly over

17

her head. Enjoying watching how she responded to it, I traced her frame with it, surveying her body to see where I was going to tap first but I wasn't done teasing her. She needed to ache for me before I tore into her. I draped the belt across the back of her thighs and told her to get acquainted with it and introduced her safe word before leaving the room to let her lay with her thoughts.

I went downstairs to smoke a cigar. While holding it between my teeth, I unbuttoned the top button of my shirt and took my cufflinks off, rolling up my sleeves in preparation of wearing her ass all the way out. I had every intention of making her worship me. When I was through with her, she'd be calling me every holy hallelujah she could think of. I pondered on whether or not I should tie my hair back, but she needed to see what a savage looked like, so I left it down. As this was her first night in training, I knew I had to introduce this life to her mildly. Because I was a bit of a sadist, I needed to gauge her pain tolerance, so I knew where her limits were. I came from a troubled background, so I knew how fine the line is and it was never my intent to abuse her. Safety was always my top priority. While it didn't look like it in the way I carried myself, I was more gentleman than savage. Looking at my watch, I put my cigar out and went back upstairs. This time, I let her hear me. Master is coming to collect what is his. When I opened the door, she was laying still like a skirt steak on a chopping block waiting to get seasoned. I could tell she was a little uncomfortable being tied up what way so I intended to untie her wrists and allow her the freedom of her arms as I would lay out my ground rules. I took the belt from her thighs and began dragging it across her legs, allowing her to kneel on the bed.

"In order to be my submissive, there are rules you must follow." I could hear a soft exhale slip from under the pillowcase I had to readjust when I came back in.

"Rule number 1: You are to address me as Daddy, Master, or Sir. I don't have a preference of which. Are those terms acceptable?" She exhaled sharply and replied "Yes..." I stretched my neck, firmly grasped hers and pinned her down. The sound of my belt hissing over her thighs and ass, and her scream that followed was soothing to me like the first drop of blood from a fresh kill touching my lips.

"I see you don't listen. Yes...what?" The power in my voice

was God-like.

"Yes, Daddy!" she exclaimed as her body curled into itself. I grinned and began to rub the spot on her body impacted by my belt.

"Good girl. Rule number 2. You are to keep a journal. In order for me to properly take care of you, I have to know what you are feeling. If what I do makes you happy, write it. If I piss you off, write it. New boundaries, write them. Concerns, write them. Are these terms acceptable to you?" She was undoubtedly enjoying herself.

"Oh my God, yes, Daddy!" she shouted. I kept a firm grip on her neck and continued to rub her down until I was ready to give her my next rule. Because this rule was so important to me, I unhanded her, untied her legs and let her sit up once again. I cut one of the lights on and raised the pillowcase so that we could see each other.

"Your safe word is "Neruda". A safe word is put in place so that boundaries are not crossed. It keeps you and I both protected. If Daddy goes past your threshold of the pain you're about to experience or oversteps your boundaries, you are to say this word and I will immediately stop as assess the situation. Repeat your safe word to me."

"Neruda…" she moaned.

"Good. Let's practice." I yanked her body closer to the edge of the bed, pulled the pillowcase back down over her head and stood over her. Leaning down over her, I began to bite her left ass cheek to gauge her pain tolerance. I gradually increased pressure. While she moaned and fidgeted, she did not utter her safe word. I applied more pressure. She moaned louder and louder, the harder I bit down until she finally screamed "Neruda!! Neruda, Daddy, Neruda…"

I immediately stopped and rubbed it. My teeth marks were embossed in her skin.

"Good girl. Let's try again, yes?" I ask. The way her breathing became heavier turned me on. My dick was harder than it was for our 44th President to get a bill passed, but I was on a mission. When she agreed to take another step, I reached under her and began to pinch her nipples. I started out with a gentle pinch, rubbing them between my fingers. The pressure became more intense until she folded her body and yelled her safe word.

"Mmmmm, that's such a good girl! Did you like that?" I celebrated. Her body was writhing in pleasure.

"Yes, Daddy! Mmmmm!" I loved to hear her moan.

"Very good. Final exercise. Ass up." As she put it in the air for me, I decided I wanted to wear her out. Pinning her back down to the bed, I swung and slapped her ass with the same concentration I first tapped her with and monitored her response. Each time I swung; I intensified the blows. She squirmed underneath my hand, but not once did she say her safe word. I paused after a few minutes because I didn't want to overload her senses. Her body wasn't familiar with what was happening to it, so it needed time to build its pain tolerance and allow the endorphins to be released and let them do what they were supposed to do. I sat in my chair watching her. Her plump ass swiveled in the air as she rocked back and forth, calling for me. I could hear the hunger in her voice as she beckoned me, yet I wouldn't answer her. Her yearning erected a power in me that would have challenged the mightiest of deities. After a few minutes of letting the chemicals in her body react, I stood back up and began again but this time, I used my hands. My palms were wide and would cover a nice portion of her ass. The difference in impact would be welcomed by her as well. While the belt would render and more precise sting, I wanted it to ripple through her body and a hand would give the desired results.

PAP!

I watched as she jolted forward but held her scream in. This round, she was different. It was as if she enjoyed the pain. She hardly made a hurtful sound, but the grunts and moans signaled to me that she liked what I was doing to her. We went through the same process: beginning from the last step and working my way harder. Each time she reacted, but she didn't speak her safe word. I made sure to study her movements and the sounds that cued her sensitivity level. I could tell the sensation of pain was beginning to come back based on the way her body squirmed all over my bed. I was waiting for 'neruda' to spill out, nonetheless, it didn't. I was astonished but very proud of her.

Pausing for a second time, I reached in between her legs to test the waters of my river and noticed she was flooding. I was pleased but I needed to drive the point home that she no longer

20

belongs to herself.

"Who told you, you could get wet?" I asked. "Clearly, you need more training." I spanked her one last time and continued to rub her pussy, alternating from fingering her to circling her clit. I could always tell when she was ready to climax, so she never had to tell me, but she surprised me when she asked for my permission to cum before I had to prompt her to. I asserted my power and told her 'No'. I knew she wouldn't be able to hold it so when she orgasmed all over my fingers, I couldn't help but grin.

"It's ok...I forgive you," I assured. I rested the spanking to, again, allow time for the chemicals and endorphins to kick it up another notch in her body. To compensate for sensation, I kept rubbing that sweet, wet flesh until she reached a second peak. I'd never seen her run from an orgasm faster than she tried to that night. My arm wrapped itself tight around her as I played with that creamy pussy until her body registered an 8.0 on the Richter Scale. I leaned into her and whispered in her ear.

"Isn't Daddy a generous Master?"

She couldn't stop squirming and moaning. It was a proud moment for me. Look at my little vixen - enjoying the pleasure I was giving her. When her body settled from her eruption, I kissed her and gave her a play session worthy of her submission. She screamed, jumped, and ran from me tagging her ass up but not once did she utter her safe word. I was thoroughly impressed. Her ass was as crimson as a Red Delicious apple with my handprints painted all over it. I kept going until her eyes glazed over. I knew she had reached subspace within her final orgasm by the way she collapsed to the bed. She panted and lay sprawled out. When I was convinced that she was completely open and fully receptive, I closed the session in a way that would change her life and our dynamic forever.

"Last rule..." I snatched the pillowcase off her head, pulled her ponytail and spoke clearly and directly into her ear.

"You no longer belong to yourself. You belong to me now. All of you. Every inch, every orgasm, every bead of sweat coming from your pores right now is mine. You will reside here. You will eat here, you will sleep in this bed, you will wash that pretty pussy of mine here. From this night on, you live with your Master. Are these terms acceptable?"

21

It sounded as if she was crying tears of joy as "yes, Daddy" slipped from her lips. This is what she had been waiting for – to be brought into my world and I loved her enough to lay waste to the saint in her and turn an angel, demon - my very own sex demon. As I gently moved her legs together so that I could lay behind her and safely bring her down from her high, my hand brushed across an incredibly huge wet spot beneath her. I chuckled to myself and began talking to her softly while holding her as her body shook. I spoke to her calmly, lightly rubbing her thighs.

"It's ok to come down. You're safe. I'm next to you. Come back to me," I said. Her body shook like she was going through withdrawals from snorting an entire kilo of cocaine to the face. After a few minutes, her breathing stopped. I paid close attention to her, lifting my head to watch her. The moonlight that crept through the blinds gave me just enough light to see her clearly. I continued to rub her body. She still hadn't taken a breath. After a few more seconds I calmly called her name.

"Mandisa. Come back to me." I said again. She gasped as if she had been just brought back to life and panted until she realized where she was. She sounded like she was under the influence of a powerful drug.

"It feels like I'm flying...Daddy, I'm flying," she mumbled. I smirked and kissed her neck before getting up.

"You're welcome." I lit a candle to help keep her tranquil. She stared into it hypnotically. Her body was limp and relaxed - her breathing steadied. When I determined she was ok and didn't need me anymore, I left the room and went back downstairs to resume catching up on sports highlights. The session kept replaying in my mind. Mandi would never be the same. She wouldn't wake up the woman she was before this night. I couldn't wait to see the phoenix in her rise from the ashes I created in destroying her. As I daydreamed, my phone rang. A huge grin stumbled on my face as I saw the number. The soft voice on the other end pulled me in.

"Hey baby girl. You missed Daddy? Good. Yea I know, baby. I've been tied up but I'm coming for you. You've been a bad girl, huh? You need punishment? I got you. I have something for you, too... a new doll...I just turned her. You'll love her. I gotta go, though. Tell your Master you love him...Good girl. I'll call you in the morning..."

CHAPTER 3
All Falls Down

Mandisa

Aziz and I had been living together for a few months now and things were seemingly perfect. We both went to work and came home every day like clockwork. He is a founding partner in a prestigious, and only Black owned law firm based in Jersey City, New Jersey and I am the editor-in-chief of a popular fashion magazine based in Newark.

During the day, I'm always so engulfed in making all the decisions – what photo to use for the cover, what articles are we going to run - top to bottom, I have the final say. Being a boss is entirely too much pressure so when I come home, I don't want the responsibility of control, which is where Aziz came in. We worked well because I have this ceaseless need to be controlled and he has a need to be in control. When I stepped through that door, I was no longer Editor-in-Chief. I was submissive to Aziz. He controlled everything that went on in our home regarding me, all the way down to what panties I was to wear each day. My primary focus was his pleasure, and I loved every single minute of it. He would come home every evening - dinner would be done, the house cleaned, and I would be sitting patiently, waiting for him to engage with me and when it was time to play, I bussed it open for him like you could find me on the hottest porn site. I was the perfect submissive, so I thought, and he always made me feel as if I was the sexiest woman alive. But as beautifully as our life weaved an admirable rug for us to stand on, one rainy evening in summer, it snatched it right from under my feet.

I got home before him that day. Since I had time to wind down a little before I started dinner, I had showered and slipped into a tank top and panties. My newest perfume was sitting on the dresser waiting for an opportunity to kiss my skin and I thought what better day than that day to break her in. I put my hair up in a messy bun, nails clacking as I finished, before heading down to the kitchen. The floor was cold under my fuzzy sock covered feet. It being too quiet for me, the first thing I did was turn my speaker on and play some music. Getting in the groove, I turned the oven to 350 and bopped to the fridge. I had no idea what I was fixing that man for dinner, so I stood there drawing a complete blank, staring at the second shelf waiting for dinner to magically appear until I remembered I had monk fish in the freezer. My R&B playlist was blasting in the speakers while I danced to the counter in a bright, chipper mood. Since the house was fairly large, I didn't hear him come in. He walked in on me singing, dancing, and chopping carrots. When I turn to go back to the fridge, I bumped right into him, jumped, and screamed because he had startled me. Both laughing, I jumped on him to welcome him home.

"Oh my God, Daddy, how long were you standing there?"

"Long enough to hear your voice crack when you tried to hit that last high note," he laughed as he put his suit jacket and briefcase on a chair. I was extremely happy to see him and the grin on my face said so.

"Whatever," I cheesed, closing the fridge, and walking back to the counter. He smiled back, came up behind me, put his hand to my throat, turning me to him and kissing me so passionately. My knees got weak as a soft moan escaped. He hadn't said a word after that. He took the bag of celery from my hand, placed it on the counter then squeezed harder around my neck before bending me over the island. It began to get hot, and it wasn't the stove. I heard his belt unbuckle and his pants unzip. As he did so, the compression around my neck became a palm covering the whole side of my face. I closed my eyes and let him have his way with me. Pulling my panties to the side, he slid his mountain hard dick into my honey well as deep as it could go and held it there. I screamed as I felt the pain shoot up my spine. He was huge. It was a wonder I was able to take all of him in. I felt my legs begin to wobble as he pounded my soft with no mercy. His hand never left my neck. He took his free hand and snatched my arm behind my back for leverage. It became a rein as he used it to push and pull my body to and from him. I listened to him grunt and groan while stroking my walls - his voice full of chaos and savagery. I took him in deeper, spacing out my legs a little bit so he could really get in there. He slapped my ass with his free hand and stroked harder. You couldn't tell me I didn't have the best pussy in the world in that moment.

His thrusts began to become longer and felt more concentrated. I knew he was about to cum. I lifted my leg over the counter, throwing it back at him as best I could, knocking the carrots over to the floor in the process. Things began to get hectic. My body repeatedly crashed into the island it was bent over, knees knocking against the cabinets. I was flinging my arms trying to get a hand on anything to help support myself. Muffled screams and animalistic growls drowned out the music playing in the background, and I came hard enough to crack the ground. My walls hugged him tighter until he un-palmed my face, gripped my hips, and shot out the biggest nut in my honey well. I was in absolute Heaven. It drove me crazy when he didn't pull out. I took my leg down and tried to catch my breath. Daddy slipped out of me, yanked me back by my throat and bit my lower jaw from the side.

"I wanted dessert first," he said as he adjusted my panties for me and smacked my ass.

"Finish up in here," he commanded. He went upstairs loosening his tie like nothing ever happened. All I could do was smile at all the diced vegetables on the floor from me trying to get my bearings straight while he fucked the living daylights out of me. We ended up ordering out that night.

Later that evening, while he sat on the couch watching tv, I sat on the other side of it quietly, awaiting any commands he may have had for me. I was reading a trashy novel when his phone rang. He looked at it briefly and set it back down on the table, face down. I looked at the time and it wasn't an hour in which a man in a committed relationship should be getting any type of calls or texts messages, however, I stayed silent. It rang again. I remained quiet, but I was curious as to who it was calling him that late. When it vibrated a 3rd time, I became annoyed and increasingly so because this time, he got up to answer in a separate room. My heart began to race, and my mind wandered. Why couldn't he speak in front of me? Who the fuck was that blowing up his phone? I couldn't understand what he was saying because he was deliberately speaking quietly, but I could hear aggression and provocation in his voice. An anger raised in me that I was unfamiliar with. I sat there in disbelief because we didn't keep secrets from each other yet there he was in another room covertly going off. I abandoned my submission the second I heard his footsteps coming as he came back to the room. My eyes and head followed him as he walked back to the couch, looking just as upset as I did.

"Who was that?" I immediately asked. He looked at me

like I had three heads as he paused before sitting down.

"Since when do we ask questions?"

"Since it's 11 o'clock, your phone is ringing off the hook and you had to leave out the room to speak to whoever it was," I snapped.

"Shut your mouth, now," he demanded rolling his eyes while turning the channel. His audacity startled and offended me. I couldn't believe it. I became infuriated as he dodged my question.

"Who was it, Aziz?"

He stared at the television, remaining silent.

"Who...was it, Aziz?" My voice began to tremble as a lump formed in my throat. Anger began to build up in his face, yet I didn't care. I needed to know. My submission is something earned, and, in that moment, he was becoming less worthy of it.

"Aziz! Who was it?!" I screamed, jumping up and throwing the book I was reading at his stiff body. He slowly turned his head, looking at me as if I disgusted him. The fury he exhibited forced a tear out of my eye. He stood up and walked towards me. I began to stumble backward until the wall interrupted my escape. Aziz continued to step towards me until I could feel the air blasting from his flared nostrils. I gasped as he put his large hand around my throat. Touching his forehead to mine, he closed his eyes, took a few deep breaths, and tore my heart out in the process.

"You do not ask questions. What I do is my business. You live in this huge house that I pay for, you drive expensive cars that I pay for, and you take this dick whenever I feel like fucking on that sweet little pussy between those legs," the pressure he applied around my neck got tighter as he spoke. His deep, steady tone struck fear in my soul.

"You do...not...ask...questions." He took a final deep breath, keeping his eyes closed, clenching his jaw before continuing.

"Are those terms acceptable?" he asked. I didn't answer. I stood there and began to sob with his forehead still to mine.

"Aziz, get off me," I cried. He let go of my neck and tried to hold me. I refused to let him. I began to fight him off me, still crying and screaming "get off me!" but he wouldn't let up.

"Mandisa...baby stop. It's nothing. That was nobody," he tried to explain. His eyes were saturated in deception. I couldn't help but to keep screaming.

"You're a liar! What have you been doing behind my back?! Who was that calling you?! Answer me, now!"

The arguing intensified. I was in disbelief as to what was happening. What was he hiding? Why couldn't he just be honest? All my questions were answered with the ringing of our doorbell. Silence fell on us as we both looked at the door. Aziz looked nervous as his body froze. The doorbell rang again. Disgust and agitation oozed over my face as I slowly turned to him.

"Aziz, who the fuck is that?" I asked, calmly. Tears began to well up in his eyes, but an answer never came from his lips. I snatched my body away from him as the betrayal began to ring louder than the doorbell. I began to back away from him like I had just found out he murdered my brother.

"Mandi...baby...don't go to that door," he said. Aziz looked uneasy as if he knew what horrible fate stood behind the front door. The lump in his throat was so big I could feel it in my own. A nauseating feeling overwhelmed me as the ringing bell turned into a banging on the door with a woman's voice on the other side screaming his name. Time stopped. Every ounce of air was instantaneously vacuumed into the abyss of treachery. I rolled my eyes, looking into the Heavens as tears began to pour down my face again. I turned to walk to the door. Aziz rushed up behind me, attempting to hug me.

"Mandisa, baby chill. Let me explain," he pleaded. I fought him off me with all my might and slapped him across his face. He was stunned as he had never seen such a fierceness in my face. Backing away, he sat down holding his head in his hands as the banging and shouting continued. I walked to the door and opened it to find a beautiful yet furious woman standing there toting a car seat with a newborn nestled, peacefully sleeping in it. She shoved it into my arms and smirked.

"Tell Daddy he left this at my house." she snapped. She dropped a baby bag and a file containing what I assumed was all the baby's records at my feet. Sound escaped me. I couldn't say a word, muster up a breath – nothing. I was in complete and utter shock looking this woman in her eyes before she stormed off. Her perfect curls and curve in her hips offended me. She violently switched her way back to a car I could have sworn Aziz just pulled out of his garage two day prior. She backed out of the driveway hastily and left me standing there with my man's newborn son. I couldn't move at first. The car seat, as light as it was, was like a ton of bricks on my arm. I remained frozen in that moment. The taillights were long gone from my sight before I was able to muster up the strength to walk back into the house.

I brought the baby and the bag inside, making sure I safely sat the car seat down before collapsing and having a full-blown panic attack. I sat there on the cold floor gasping for air. My head began to pound, and my palms became clammy with sweat. It felt like I was dying inside. I kept imagining her in my head. She was so beautiful it made the betrayal 10 times worse. She looked about his age as he was a couple of years older than me so it looked like she would have been a better fit for him. The shooting pain in my head blinded me. I sobbed and gasped simultaneously as reality brought me back to Earth. There was no fresh air around me to breathe in as it became polluted with sedition. Aziz rushed to me and wrapped me tight in his arms. I soaked his shirt in tears. I didn't even have the muscle to fight him anymore.

Aziz

I fucked up. Bad. I loved Mandisa from the moment I laid eyes on her. Even told her I was going to marry her one day, the very first day I met her, but I had secrets that came spilling out that just ruined everything I was building towards. That bitch. I had always preferred polyamorous relationships, but I never wanted Mandisa to find out this way. She didn't deserve any of it.

I was relaxing in the den with Mandisa next to me waiting to be told what to do. It had to be about 11 o'clock when my phone first rang. Normally, my phone is on Do Not Disturb but I had an important case I was working on that required my full availability. When I picked the phone up and saw who it was, I kept my shock to myself and placed the phone back on the table face down. I didn't even give it a second thought. Then the phone vibrated again. I continued flipping through the channels trying to calm down while simultaneously pretending as if I don't hear the loud vibration coming from my phone. I didn't even look in Mandisa's direction. I could already tell it was going to be a problem. A couple of minutes went by after the phone stopped ringing. I thought that was the end of it. I had settled on an old sitcom but before I could really get into it, the phone went off again. Clearly, the person calling needed my attention but because of who that person was, I couldn't answer in front of Mandi. I scoffed, grabbing the phone and went to my bedroom. I made sure Mandi wasn't behind me before closing the door and answering it.

"Tyra what do you want? You know you can't be callin' me like this...I know it's been a minute, Babygirl, but I'm working on it...No, I haven't told...I know what I said...you getting' outta pock...Tyra...you'd better not...Tyra, I'm done arguing with... Tyra..."

After the third time of me saying her name and she not listening, I hung up on her and cut my phone off – important case be damned. She wasn't going to harass me all night. It was bad enough I had to speak to her in a hushed tone so Mandi wouldn't hear, but if she thought I was about to go back and forth with her, she had another thing coming.

Tyra was my first submissive. We had a long history with each other. We could never really be together as a couple, but her pussy was so good, I just couldn't let her go. She always wanted to be in a relationship with me yet, I could never see myself with her. She was beautiful - almost as tall as me, slender but curvy, and light skinned with green eyes. She had freckles that looked like a map of the stars and long, jet black hair I loved to pull on. But... she just couldn't be the one for me. When I met Mandisa, Tyra and I were on a "break". At the time, she was struggling with her submission, breaking my rules left and right so I decided that she needed time to herself to gather her thoughts. It had been years in the making, at this point, because she was never really capable of submitting – the whole "I don't bow to anybody" banter those independent women scream all the time. Our inevitable end had shown itself on the horizon, but it wasn't over. About 3 months into my relationship with Mandi, Tyra and I reconnected, and she ended up pregnant. While I told her about Mandi, I didn't tell Mandi about her, and it made her upset. Throughout her entire pregnancy, she questioned me about when I was going to leave Mandi and come be with her, "where I was supposed to be". She would trip out and go ballistic, threatening to tell Mandi every-thing all the time. To simmer her down, I'd go to her, give her the dick and attention she needed and smother the flames she tried to ignite. When she went into labor with my son, I lied to Mandi, telling her I had to leave for a business trip, and I'd be gone for a few days. She never thought twice about it, and it worked perfectly because Tyra lived far enough to where I didn't have to be worried if someone could spot me. My son was born at her home. I paid for doulas, midwives, and cucumbers for her eyes after the birth because according to her, the lack of sleep she experienced caused bags under them and that's what she wanted. I spared no expense. Afterall, she was still my submissive. I saw my son every week. Mainly due to my schedule, but also because I still hadn't figured out how to tell Mandi.

Fast forward 3 months, Tyra became increasingly posses-sive, often using my son as a pawn to get my attention. We began arguing often because I wouldn't leave Mandi or at least tell her that she was in the picture. She would even threaten to keep my son from me like I wouldn't throw every judge at her with the level

31

of pull I had in the judicial circuit. It got to the point where I had to stop accepting her phone calls. It all came to a head the night she started blowing up my phone.

When I came to sit back down, Mandi asked who it was. I knew it was about to be some shit, but I had to play it off like I wasn't worried about shit she was talkin' about. My subs don't ask questions and that's what I intended to stick to. Mandi wasn't having it though. She immediately and sharply called me out. When she asked a second time who it was, I started to get irritated and told her to shut her mouth. I didn't want to have to lie to her, so I tried to evade the question at all costs – couldn't even look at her. Her eyes would have seen right through the lie I was so desperately trying to mask. Mandi became so irate that she jumped up and threw a book at me demanding I tell her who it was. A spirit of rage set over me as I rose from my chair and approached her. She stumbled backward, nearly curling up the wall. Seeing the fear in my shorty's eyes broke me but I had to reaffirm dominance, or I would lose her submission. I could feel my heart racing, about to beat itself out of my chest. I could feel the heat permeating from her face as her throat found its way into the grip of my hand and I touched my forehead to hers in attempt to connect with her. She was livid and I knew if lies came out of my mouth she would never trust me again, so I danced around the truth like it had challenged me to a battle on the yard.

"You do not ask questions. What I do is my business. You live in this huge house that I pay for, you drive expensive cars that I pay for, and you take this dick whenever I feel like fucking on that sweet little pussy between those legs," I growled. I didn't know what else to say. It was my last-ditch effort to get her to forget about my phone ringing off the hook. It failed miserably. She began bawling, trying to push me off of her yet I tried holding her tight. I struggled with telling her it was nothing because she knew I wasn't truthful. My nerves started showing up in my voice, trembling like weak knees standing on a tight rope over the Grand Canyon. The more she screamed, the tighter I tried to hold her. Hearing her call me a liar snatched my entire spinal cord through my chest. Every ounce of dominance in me knelt at her feet in surrender as I pleaded with her to let me explain. I allowed her to yell, push me off her and say some of the harshest words I never expected to come from her gut. Even though she had every right to, the words were like daggers in my eardrums. It hurt but it wasn't as painful as the sound of the doorbell interrupting her fury. I'll never forget the shocking sadness in her face as we locked eyes while the doorbell rang again. I had to have looked like a sick puppy dog. We both realized I was caught at the same time and an instant calm came to her.

"Aziz, who the fuck is that?" she asked. It was a wrap at the point. She jerked away from me and started backing away from me like I had leprosy. I told her not to go to the door like I still had any authority. She looked at me with such disgust. She began sobbing again yet no sound came from her. Each ring of the doorbell made her jump like she was being stung by bee after bee until the ringing became banging and Tyra began shouting. Mandi turned to open the door, so I quickly rushed behind her trying to prevent her from going further. She followed up with the strength of ten men and broke free from me, slapping me directly across the face. I didn't know what to say. What could I say? The white flag rose and waved as I retreated to couch, completely defeated.

"Tell Daddy he left this."
I could hear that bitch from the den. All I needed Tyra to do was relax a lil bit and I would have taken care of it all! We could have been a happy family had I been given the opportunity to do things my way! But no. She wanted to be Mandi so bad. Bad enough to force the ending of my relationship with her. How was I going to salvage this? I couldn't lose Mandi. She gave me a sense of belonging I couldn't find anywhere else. She gave me purpose. I craved to be needed and she needed me. Minutes felt like years before she came back into the den. She moved like a zombie, with my son in tow. Her face was emotionless. She carefully put the car seat down before falling to the floor. Staring into it, she sat in silence. I was too afraid to say anything. It looked like she was in a daze but rose from the dead as she took a deep breath and started crying and hyperventilating. I rushed to console her, holding her in my arms. What did I do? How could I let this happen? No level of defense or articulately structured plea bargain was going to get me off of Death Row with this. I needed to just come clean, fess up and own my shit...

Mandisa

"Baby, I'm sorry. I fucked up. Daddy fucked up. Let me make it up to you," he begged. He ran his fingers through my hair in attempt to console me, trying to promise me that it'll all be ok. I wanted to believe him – even tried to. But the pain I was experiencing over his duplicity and, let's be honest, his audacity was devastating. There I was, a woman that laid the stars in my eyes at his feet and commanded them to worship him, being reduced to just another woman giving her all and getting cheated on in return. There were so many emotions streaming through my body, but I instantaneously became numb when the sound of a crying baby filled the room. Aziz let go as I pushed off him. I had no more tears to cry. I slowly scooted over to the car seat and pulled the baby blanket back to reveal a fussy little replica of the man I was so madly in love with that I didn't give him.

A baby boy. He was so tiny and precious – looked just like his father. I put my anger to the side and unstrapped him to hold him in my arms. The little body stretched as a yawn fluttered out and crying continued. The shards of my broken heart melted as I almost began to swoon over him. I sat there cradling and trying to comfort my Dominant's lies and deceit in my arms. When he would not settle, I pulled a bottle from the baby bag and began to feed him while I rocked him, singing to him so sweetly. My voice was weak and full of sadness. The only strength my body had was enough to hold him steady in my arms. I rocked him and sang until he fell back to sleep. When he drifted off, I placed him in Aziz's arms and got up to pack my things. I saw him, out of my peripheral, look up as his eyes followed me out of the den. I didn't utter a word to him on the way out. Tiptoeing unnecessarily up the stairs, I gathered all of my essential belongings, leaving everything else and headed back down to the front door. As I looked back, Aziz was still on the floor with the baby in one arm and his free hand covering his eyes with his head leaned back.

Fortunately, I never sold my condo but kept it as rental property for a popular short stay vacation company, so I had somewhere to go. I blocked off the rest of my calendar, went home and

34

didn't look back. I drove home in silence and completely numb. The light from oncoming traffic hurt my eyes due to all the tears that fell from them. It's a wonder I made it there safely considering I truly was not paying attention to the road. As I pulled up into my parking spot, I heaved a heavy sigh. I pulled myself into the front door, to the elevator and into my home.

I'd forgotten what the sound of my locks were like. My hand trembled turning the key. Dread swallowed me whole as I opened the door. Cutting the lights felt like someone blew powdered glass into my eyes. Squinting, I found my way into my bedroom. I didn't even bother showering. When I collapsed on the bed, face up, I stared into the ceiling and cried like a ba...I cried profusely. After giving myself a headache, I got up to cut the light off and lit a candle, after which, I undressed and laid back down. The thought of what life was now going to be like stormed through my mind. Flashes of him making love to me came up. Quick images of the way his palms perfectly slapped my ass surfaced. As I lay there, hours later, his juices finally began to gush from my honey well. I always loved that feeling until then. An incredible amount of grief came over me. What the fuck was I going to do now? I needed a Dominant to even me out. How was I going to get the things I need? I resolved that I had to put me first.

Aziz never heard from me again after that night. My heart was shattered into a million pieces. I loved him with everything I had - submitted to him with my entire being. What he did was a crime that I could never forgive. I simply had to just move on, but one thing was for certain:

I could *NEVER* go back to a vanilla life.

CHAPTER 4
Tabula Rasa (A Clean Slate)

Mandisa

It took me 7 and a half months to get Aziz out of my sys-
tem. We had been in this lifestyle for a while and I had gotten used
to things being a certain way so when it all stopped as abruptly as
it did, it forced me into this foggy space I couldn't get myself out
of. I ached for the welts. I yearned for the bruises. I craved the bite
marks in my flesh. The choking, the spanking, the lack of being
controlled by another person would all come crashing down on
me in the night to the point of where I could not function properly
during the day. A sweeping depression cocooned my soul yet the
butterfly that lie inside was dead.

Aziz tried to get in contact with me for months after I left
but I never responded. My email inbox was flooded. He'd text
me long, drawn out paragraphs about "how sorry he was" and
how he "never meant to hurt me" and I would leave him on read
every time. The man even called every now and again, probably
in hopes that I'd at least answer that time. I never did. He knew
what he had done was the ultimate sin. Though I had given up on
him, I couldn't help but wonder who the woman that destroyed my
dynamic was. Was she another submissive he had tucked away?
Were they in a formal relationship? My heart shattered every time I
thought about it. To keep me from losing myself in the memory of
his transgression, I had to keep my mind busy, so I enveloped myself with work. We were revealing the new cover for next month's
issue and because of who it was, we had to release it in grand fashion. I called on my assistant to help plan a launch party.

Trinity was my right hand in all things. She was so involved with my life that she eventually became my best friend. She
was in her office arguing with a photographer over double booking
when I walked up to the door.

"What don't you understand about priority clients?! We
are the biggest, Black WOMAN owned magazine on this side
of the country! You don't mistakenly double book yourself for a
shoot when you have one with us first! Call me back when you've
rescheduled your other client," she freaked. Hanging up on the
photographer, she inhaled and exhaled deeply trying to calm down.

"Hey girl," she said. I chuckled.

"Hey boo," I responded as I sat on her desk. "You ok in here? Sounds like people are pissing you off again."

"Girl, I'm fine. I just hate stupid shit. How do you double book clients on us? We book with you on the same day every single month. How do you make a mistake like that? I just don't get it," she confessed.

"So, what are we going to do?"

"We...aren't going to do anything. They're going to reschedule their other client and honor the commitment they made to us," she retorted. She was so annoyed. I got a kick out of how much fire could come from such a small person.

"Well, what's up with the launch party? Have you found a venue yet?" I asked.

"Oh yea! I meant to talk to you about that. I found this sexy club downtown called Rasa. I looked at it and booked with the owner on the spot. It was too fly to pass up and the best part about it is we're still under budget for a venue!"

"My girl," I cheered, giving her a high five. We spoke about logistics a little more but then the conversation went left.

"But girl let me tell you about the owner with his fine ass. I had to make sure the girls were sitting up nicely while we spoke," she said as she pushed her breasts up in her blouse. I laughed and shook my head.

"Ok well just make sure you and the girls have everything on lock before this release party. We have potential investors coming and everything needs to be perfect."

"What's my name, bitch?"

"Trinnie"

"Say it again, hoe!"

"Trinnie, heffa."

"Ok then...how have you been doin' today though? You know I have to check in with you every day," she inquired.

"I've seen better days, babe. But I'm ok," I assured her.

"Aziz still calling you? You haven't really spoken to me about him as of late."

"Not in a while. I guess he finally got a clue," I said.

"I know that's right. Fuck 'em girl. I know he's somewhere laid up in a fetal position after losing you. As devoted as you were

39

to him. All the cooking and cleaning you did. All the kinky shit you allowed to go on. Girl, I still don't know how you did it. That's some crazy shit, bitch."

"Yea well, that's his business," I said, brushing her comment off. I tried to hide the fact that my spirit dwindled upon hearing it, but I don't think it worked. Trinnie saw gloom come over me and quickly changed the subject.

"Drinks later? It is $2 Tuesdays at Jomo's!" she exclaimed. I knew she was trying to cheer me back up, but I had no intentions of going out that night or any other night besides the release party. I had become a real Debbie Downer since the split. The slight tension was interrupted by my receptionist knocking on the door frame, telling Trinnie the photographer was back on the line. Scoffing, she picked up her phone and told him he'd better have confirmation of our scheduled shoot. Her attitude was top tier. I giggled and shook my head, leaving her office to head back to mine. I sat quietly at my desk, staring at the space where a picture of Aziz and I once rested. A small succulent in a gold pot had taken its place but it didn't bring me as much joy as the picture once did. Nevertheless, being a new plant mom gave me peace. The rest of the day went smoothly: all photoshoots booked, all articles met deadlines, Trinnie didn't kill anybody - smoothly.

As the end of the workday approached, I closed down my laptop, packed my briefcase and headed towards the door. A few of my employees were still on the clock so I bid them adieu and stayed focused on the exit. The parking lot was dark, damp, and cold. My pace began to quicken at the sight of my truck. I just couldn't wait to get home. Though the day was easy, it was also long, and my feet had had enough. There were a couple of people conversing in the parking lot and when our eyes met, we explained pleasantries. As I unlocked the door, I spotted them still looking my way. It wasn't in a threatening manner but more like they were wondering who I was getting into my whip. I chuckled to myself and hopped in.

I always got a kick out of people's reactions when they saw me and my small frame hop in and out of such a big body truck, and God knows I whipped Pitch Black around like I knew a little something about what I was doing. I cranked up my Trap music playlist, put my shades on and backed out of my space. Exiting out of the garage, the daylight was still beaming. I opened my sunroof along with all of the windows and let the air flow through. The music blasting summoned my inner trap queen and the most gangster of faces washed over me. Dramatically bopping in the driver's seat, I became the biggest drug dealer in town in my mind.

When I got home and tapped the key card over the lobby door sensor, the universe thought it would be a funny joke to play on me as I caught a whiff of cologne on a passerby. It was the same scent Aziz wore. An overwhelming feeling of anxiety stirred immediately. The air was thick, I lost my breath, the lobby began to spin, and I started to spiral. The concierge quickly jumped up to aide me, asking me if I was alright. I told him I was fine as I fought hard to keep back oceans of tears, making my way to the elevator, supporting myself with its back wall. I heaved as the doors closed. Closing my eyes, it took everything in me not to just scream. Why couldn't I just let go? It had been 7 and a half months. Surely his impact couldn't be that strong still. I quickly snatched my phone from my purse and called Mozelle, my good friend and certified sex therapist. I was frantic.

"Hey Sexiness!" she answered. My breathing was still labored as I made my way to my door.

"Mozelle...I...I... help...please...," I panted.

"Whoa! Whoa! Mandi, calm down! What's wrong?"

"I don't know! I caught a whiff of...his cologne...and I just...I panicked!" I dropped to the floor with my back to the door, holding my forehead. Sweat began to pour from my neck and palms. My chest hurt from gasping for air.

"Ok ok! Are you home yet? I'm coming up right now!" she said. Mozelle lived 2 floors below me, so it was relatively easy for her to get to me in case of an emergency. I crawled away from the door so that she could get in. Like a true friend, she rushed to my aid. Sitting with me, she coached my breathing - 'breathe in through the nose, 1-2-3, exhale through the mouth'. Closing my eyes, I tried to match her. It was so hard to achieve. The scent clung to my nostrils for dear life and wouldn't die.

Mozelle sat there with me until my breathing regulated, and I could calm down. I started to feel cold - almost uncommunicative. I stared at the floor as images of the woman that tore my home apart flashed in my mind. I saw the look of malice she wore on her face. I saw the baby's beautiful face. I heard his crying. I could smell the newborn on him. The heartbroken submissive inside me forced a single tear down my face. It was the only way I could say that I was still hurting. I was so lost in those tormenting thoughts that I didn't even hear Mozelle calling to me. Her voice was soft as drugstore cotton.

"Mandi? Can you hear me? Where are you?" she called. My eyes shifted to hers, but my body remained completely still. Tears began to flow faster until I just started to cry uncontrollably. Mozelle held me close to her, consoling me. I mustered up enough strength to hold onto her as I cried.

After I drained both eyes of all tears for the next ten years, Mozelle helped me up off the floor. I sat on the couch while she made some tea. Sitting there in a daze, I listened to the whistling of the tea kettle. It was hypnotic. I slowly curled myself into a ball and allowed my surroundings to comfort me. The tea kettle, the cool air, the rays from the last bit of sunlight before it set peering through the window - I felt like the universe was back on my side at that moment.

Mozelle came back with 2 mugs, handing me one. It was perfect: chamomile, with a spoonful of pure honey. My hands hugged the mug like a long-lost friend. I felt Mozelle's hand rub my foot.

"What happened, Bunny?" she asked. "Bunny" was her nickname for me as she was always "Bully". She and I had a unique dynamic between us. I was always the soft, quiet, and meek one whereas she was always aggressive and often passed as mean... like a pit bull. She was a beautiful, tall, and milk chocolate woman with natural, curly hair she always kept pinned up into a neat, delicate fro-hawk, and the most hypnotizing brown eyes you could ever look into - full of divine femininity.

"I don't know, Bully. I thought I was over it or at least getting close to it, and then I got the scent of his cologne in my nose and completely lost it. I don't understand it. How could he still have such a hold on me like this?" I asked. She, being a certified sex therapist made things a little easier to understand.

"Well, when you devote yourself to somebody in such a way as you have, those soul ties become incredibly strong. You're not just dealing with a physical connection. You battle a spiritual and mental bond as well. Those are the toughest to break and it's unfortunate that his indiscretions yanked the rug from under your feet without the proper footing you needed to still be able to stand." Bully played no games when it came to my heart. It was so energizing that she knew and understood what I was dealing with. This lifestyle isn't for the faint of heart and most people will not understand it.

"Well, what now? It's been almost 8 months. I need to get out of this funk. I'm trying to process and understand this space I'm in. Is this still considered subspace?" I asked. Bully chuckled.

"I don't think so, Bunny. Subspace is a place of euphoria. Subspace feels good. It's all your hormones going into overdrive causing feelings of a high, of sorts, ya know? What you're experiencing is depression and anxiety from not having access to a lifestyle that made you feel amazing. Subspace shouldn't leave you feeling depressed. It should at some point give you a boost of energy and it definitely doesn't last damn near 8 months. Does that make sense?" she lectured.

"Yea, I guess you're right. I just didn't know shit like this could affect a person so much," I said.

"It's like that, babe. BDSM is no ordinary lifestyle. It involves a massive amount of trust, devotion, and discipline. It's truly a responsibility and if your Dominant doesn't understand that then it's best you walk away. You did the right thing in leaving, Bunny. He was supposed to be accountable for your physical, mental, and spiritual wellbeing and he failed. He didn't deserve your submission. Bastard."

You could almost see the steam start to rise from her scalp, she was so upset. She had a look of disgust on her face so defined, a sculptor would have loved to use her as a muse. We sat, curled up on opposite ends of the couch in brief silence. My phone rang. It was Trinnie. Putting the phone on speaker, I answered, sounding so down and out.

"Hey girl," I moped.

"Bitch GET'CHO shit together and let's go! I told you it's $2 Tuesdays and yo' ass don't need to be in the house!" she yelled.

43

Mozelle immediately jumped up, putting the mug on the coffee table, leaving me no room to decline.

"Yup! We'll be there, Trinnie! I'm getting her dressed right now!" she exclaimed. I had the best friends. They always knew how to make things right in my life. Mozelle took the mug from my hand, placed it on the table and yanked me off the couch.

"Heffa, let's go. You don't have anything to do in the morning but make decisions at a big ass desk," she said. I softly laughed, shook my head, and followed her to my bedroom. She was already in my closet picking out my outfit by the time I got there. I undressed and cut the shower on. Watching her lay my clothes on the bed, I shook my head harder at her excitement for us to be going out. She tapped me on my bare ass and kissed my cheek.

"Get ready, hoe! I'm going downstairs to do the same. I'll be back up in 45 minutes and I swear to God when I get up here, you'd better be dressed and ready to go!" she scolded.

"Yes, ma'am," I laughed as she skipped her happy ass down the hall and to her apartment. I heaved a weighty sigh and started my shower. The bathroom steamed up quickly as I stepped inside the copper-colored hotbox. Surprisingly, the tile was still cold. I rested on the wall for a few seconds, allowing the scalding hot water to run down my back. It felt so good, I leaned my head back into it and let it cascade through my hair. It coiled up as the moisture saturated it. I washed it quickly then began to rub my body. The shampoo running down my back and into my ass felt like silk. I didn't take long considering I hadn't much time to lollygag, so I washed all the important parts and stepped out onto the navy blue, plush bathroom rug and grabbed my towel.

After the shower, I dried off and began getting dressed. Mozelle picked out a cute mustard yellow crop top and a pair of grey skinny jeans for me to wear. I rubbed my favorite lotion over my body and inhaled. The scent of grapefruit tickled my nostrils - the smell always got me excited. Clasping my bra, I noticed how it made my breasts looked divine and made a note to myself to go back and purchase a few more on my next free day. I slid a matching thong on and modeled in the mirror. My body was exquisite. "How could anyone fumble the bag on me?", I thought. Once I put my clothes and shoes on, I headed towards the door with my purse and keys. Part of me felt like leaving my cell phone at home because I truly didn't want to be bothered but I'd decided it was in my best interest to stuff it in my bag as I walked out just in case.

I met Mozelle downstairs at her place. She was just putting her jeans on when I got there. I sat on her couch while she finished getting ready. The music was blasting in "pre-turn up" fashion. Watching her dance around filled my spirit with joy. She was always so lively. Mozelle was never one to shy away from a good time. Her energy became contagious as I began dancing while still seated on the couch. Trap music was always the go-to when we wanted to get hyped up for the night. As I discreetly twerked on her couch, she came out of her room with her tongue sticking out as she danced, fully dressed and ready to go. I laughed while dancing harder and getting up to leave. We made it to her car cackling and talking shit the whole way down. My energy felt lifted and my burden lighter.

On the race there, Mozelle sparked her joint. She took two pulls and handed it to me, but I declined as weed really wasn't my thing.

"Bitch, take this shit and stop playin' with me,' Mo snapped. I chuckled and took it from her to avoid confrontation. As I took my first pull, I closed my eyes, laid my head back and exhaled slowly, letting it pass narrowly between my lips. The sound of Mo's bracelets jingling from her dancing in the driver's seat filled the air. It sounded like a tambourine against the music blasting. I took another pull. It didn't take long for the greenery to take effect. Mozelle always had the strongest weed. As I start feeling myself float, a hazy smile came over my face. I handed Mo's herbal sorcery back to her and giggled to myself. I turned my head and we caught eyes. She let out the biggest laugh.

"Daaaamn, you only had two pulls! You're such a light-weight!'

"No bitch, it's something extra in that shit," I refute.

"Yea hoe! That Don't Give a Fuck!" she laughed as she took two more pulls before putting it out. We laughed and danced the rest of the way in true hot girl fashion.

When we pulled up to Jomo's, the line was incredibly long. God knows I wasn't prepared to stand there and wait. Fortunately, Trinnie made it before us and was waiting for us at the door with a tall, dark, and absolutely gorgeous man who I'm going to assume was security standing next to her. She spotted us as soon as the valet pulled off. Patting Tall & Dark excitedly on his arm, she pointed to us then waved us over. I swear Trinnie knew somebody everywhere she went. As we walked up, he opened the rope and let us in. Trinnie smiled, stood on her toes, grabbed him by his face and licked him from his chin to nose.

"I swear to God, I'm going to suck the soul out of your dick later," she said. He smiled and smacked her on the ass before reaching in his wallet for his credit card.

"You and your girls go have a good time, baby. I'll see you later," he responded, handing her a set of keys. Trinnie grinned from ear to ear before turning around and skipping into the club, braids bouncing the entire way. We followed looking ridiculously confused.

"Trinnie, who is that?!" I asked.

"Oh girl, that's my personal trainer. I fuck him regularly though. Dude's got a fuckin' elephant trunk between his legs, I swear," she informed as she strutted her way through the second door.

All Mozelle could do was shake her head as we trailed behind.

"I told you this bitch was a witch," she laughed. Not only did Tall & Dark hand Trinnie his whole life, but he also had a section blocked off for us so that we could turn up in peace. I don't know what kind of voodoo she was putting on that man, but I wasn't about to ask questions either.

The music was loud. You could feel the vibrations from the bass in the seats. Jomo's was a mix between classy and punk. There were crystal chandeliers hanging from the ceiling and black-light graffiti on the walls. Surprisingly, the air within the space was relatively cool considering the number of people there. It was packed for it to be a Tuesday but the DJ spinning that night always drew a crowd. Trinnie booked him for the cover release party as well, so I got a chance to see how good his work was. He definitely had the people jumping so that was a plus for me.

As the night carried on, we threw back drink after drink and danced to song after song. The alcohol eased the pain in my feet from the heels I had on so you couldn't tell me anything. After a while, we ended up on the dance floor with everybody else. Whenever we went out, we were always each other's "girlfriend" so that men wouldn't press us too much. As Trinnie was dancing in her own little world, Mozelle and I danced closely to each other. We giggled and shouted as the DJ played hit after hit. A few songs went by before he started to mellow down for the night with some slow jams.

The air became thick at this point. All the body heat from people dancing made it swelter. Mozelle and I locked eyes as we danced back toward each other. A wave of consciousness passed through me, and I suddenly became fully aware of where I was. As I connected with Mo, I immediately felt an attraction to her that I never felt before. I'm not sure if it was all the weed and tequila or the fact that I hadn't had an orgasm in months, but my friend was looking so sexy to me. She stared back at me as if she was envisioning me naked. Her tongue was poking out through a devilish grin.

As we danced slowly against each other, her fingertips traced my arms until her hands were locked with mine. Her eyes were closed, and her head swayed back to the music. The definition in her cheekbones called to me. I could see exactly where I wanted to bite. I watched her breasts as her chest heaved from breathing. Even after all that dancing, she still smelled like Sunday morning. Every bit of my fiber as a human being wanted to let my tongue show her body how to really dance. What was happening? Why was I feeling this way about my friend? All of those questions were laid to rest as I felt her lips press against mine.

Our kiss was magical. Her lips were soft like my soul could lay there and drift to peaceful sleep. My eyes slowly and heavily closed as if I was in a trance. I felt her left-hand slide around to the small of my back, her right cupped my face. Our tongues met. It was almost like they had already known each other the way they hugged. We got lost in the moment. In the chaos we stood in, there was no one on the dance floor but she and I and I enjoyed every second of it. As soon as I felt myself getting lost, we were forcefully split apart by the sound of Trinnie's loud exclaim.

"Ooooooh shit!" she yelled. Mozelle and I were visibly embarrassed. Trinnie put her arms around both of our shoulders with a huge grin on her face.

"I knew you bitches were gonna go at it sooner or later," she affirmed. Mozelle's eyes wandered as I looked down at my feet. Trinnie continued:

"So ya'll gon' act like that didn't just happen? Ok whatever. That's ya'll missing out. I'm about to go get this pussy tossed to the wind by that amazing specimen of a man right there so... I'll talk to you hoes later. I'll holla!" as she threw up a peace sign and traipsed off. Mo and I both bashfully chuckled.

"You ready to go?" she asked. I hesitated to answer. Still nervous and confused about what just happened.

"Uuh...yea sure." We grabbed our things and headed to the door leaving the rest of the unsuspecting crowd behind.

The ride home was uncommonly awkward. The silence was louder than a sonic boom in my heart. Once we pulled into the parking lot, Mozelle let out a huge sigh. I think she was grateful we made it back alive with her drunk driving. As we stumbled our way to the door, laughter erupted.

"Hey, did you see that guy with the turquoise suit on? I'm trying to figure out who he thought he was," she said. My laughter followed.

"Girl, I don't know but clearly he was trying to hire some hoes tonight,"

We tripped our way to the elevator and pressed our respective floors. The ride up was no different than the ride home. The discomfort was heavy. We both looked up at the ceiling trying not to look at each other. We stopped on Mo's floor first. As the doors opened and she headed out, she looked back at me with longing in her eyes. They invited me but when I didn't follow, disappointment shrouded her face. She dropped her head slightly and tried to smile.

"I'll check on you tomorrow, boo" as she backed out. She stood there as the doors closed, our eyes connected the entire time. On my way up, my mind became a storm. Question after question about what just occurred blew passed. When I got to my apartment door, part of me started aching to call her to talk about it. I resisted the urge and left it alone. I placed my keys on the entry console and stepped out of my shoes, leaving them right at the floor. I let out a heavy sigh while scratching my head. I began taking my clothes off leaving each article on the floor in a trail leading to my bedroom.

I started a shower, trying to clear my mind as the water ran down my back, but images of my friend kept flashing through my mind. All the possibilities swam around my brain like a school of fish swimming out to further seas. The softness of her lips, the heat radiating from her body - it all overwhelmed me. I had never been with a woman before, so I was both reluctant and intrigued at the same time. I kept thinking about what her pussy looked like, what it would taste like. Would I like it? Would I even be good at it? I thought about what getting my pussy tasted by another woman would be like. Is the myth really true that women eat it better than men? I envisioned her tongue circling my clit as my hands made their way down to it. I closed my eyes and let my fingertips start doing the work. I focused hard on the feeling with Mozelle in the center of my thoughts but as soon as I was about to climax, I stopped abruptly and caught my breath. I couldn't go through with it. That was my friend. It was a friendship that was then possibly ruined. I kept my hands to myself and washed away the sweat from the evening along with the lust I was feeling for her.

I dried off, put my sleeping shirt on and climbed into bed though I knew I wouldn't be getting any rest. I was too anxious to sleep, and my overthinking would cause me to analyze every single second of that kiss and the moments afterwards. I laid there with my eyes wide open staring at the ceiling. What was I going to say to her in the morning? How were we going to get past this? My thoughts were interrupted by my doorbell. I lifted my head up, then looked at the clock. I didn't move. I sat there listening intently to make sure I even heard a doorbell ring. Seconds later, it rang again. I get up this time and head to the door. I looked through the peephole and felt my heart drop to my ankles when I saw Mozelle on the other side. I paused, unlocked the door, and opened it. Mozelle flung herself through it, grabbed my face and kissed me so passionately.

I heard the door slam behind us, and I was backed up against the wall. She kissed my neck softly then bit down aggressively. I gasped. My hands started to explore her body as she continued to kiss mine. I lifted her night shirt, grazed my fingernails up her back and felt her get a chill. We kissed again. I could feel my soft begin to get wet. Mozelle's hands were warm as they delicately wandered up my shirt. She gripped my ass as she bit my bottom lip. There were no words exchanged at all but we both communicated with each other effortlessly in that moment.

My knees began to get weak as she pulled my shirt over my head and began sucking on my left nipple. My arms were restrained above my head, and I was halfway blindfolded as Mozelle didn't completely take the shirt off

"Mozelle," I whimpered. "What is happening right now? We can't do this." Mozelle continued to suck. At that moment, she was no longer Mozelle.

"Bully, please," I pleaded. She stopped and pulled the shirt from over my eyes, tossing it to the floor.

"Bully please, what?" she asked softly. Her eyes pierced mine as I stood there naked, still backed against the wall. She pressed her body firmly up against mine, grabbed my face with one hand and slid two fingers from her other down to my clit. I moaned.

"Please...what?" she asked again. She held onto my bottom lip with her teeth as she circled my honey pot and listened to the moans and whimpers that came from me. The cold wall had lost its frigidness in the wake of my body temperature rising. Because my body had already been stimulated from me halting my orgasm a few minutes prior, it didn't take long for me to cum. My body shook as I reached my climax. I covered my own mouth in fear of screaming too loud. As I came down, I saw a smile come across her face as she nudged her head toward my bedroom. I timidly obliged. I still hadn't fully grasped what was going on, but I liked it.

I laid down on my bed, still shy, still afraid. My legs were closed as if I had no clue what was going to happen next. Bully stood at the foot of the bed and stared at me for a second. Grabbing both ankles, she spread my legs and crawled in between. My back arched like a perfect rainbow when I felt her warm, wet, soft tongue caress my clit. Juices had already begun to flow from my time backed up against the wall, so as I felt them running down my ass, I was not shocked.

Her tongue felt like a cloud enveloping my sweet spot, pulsing over and over. My moans got louder with every flick, roll and wave. It definitely reigned true in that moment that women eat pussy better than men because I swear Aziz could never. I felt her slide 2 fingers inside my gushing well and curl them like she was beckoning my soul to come out from the shadows. I immediately begin to orgasm. My soul felt like it was lifting from my body, the way the energy rushed over me. I shook violently. I tried to push Bully's head away, but she pulled her fingers out, gripped my thighs and continued eating. I snatched the sheets, leaving the bare mattress exposed in some parts of the bed.

After I exploded, my body fell completely limp. I laid there heaving and full of joy. Bully climbed up my body and kissed me passionately. I tasted myself all in her mouth. While we kissed, I caressed her body, slowly lowered my hand and reaching under her night shirt. I allowed my middle finger to get familiar with her clit. She paused briefly as if she was trying to process whether or not it was really happening. She was super wet, and her moans were melodic.

I pushed up off of the bed to where we were both sitting up and I pulled her shirt up over her head. I softly ran my fingers through her hair then firmly gripping a handful of it as I bit down on her neck. Not letting go of either, I slowly laid her body down. I didn't know I had such dominance in me. She then called to me.

"Bunny. You know what you're doing?" she asked. She knew I had never eaten pussy before but based on her tone, she was asking in a way to make sure I was fully aware and cognizant of what I was about to try and accomplish.

"I'll figure it out along the way down. Let me know when I get it right," I suggested. I licked her from neck to earlobe before letting go of her ear. I watched her briefly as she heavily breathed and bit her bottom lip. Her eyes were closed, and her arms were above her head. The tip of my tongue playfully danced around her nipples. I observed her reaction to it. She was smiling and licking her lips. I felt her fingers run through my hair as she looked at me.

"That feels good, Bunny. Don't stop," she whispered, and I didn't. I kissed and licked my way all the way down. I took a play out of the book of Aziz when I got down to her thighs. I licked her right thigh, making a trail to her left. I went by way of her clit, however, when I passed it, I barely grazed it with my tongue and watched the anticipation in her rise. I teased her a little bit longer. When I felt she couldn't take anymore, I dived, tongue first into her pussy.

51

Mozelle

Mandisa is full of shit. She said she had never been with
a woman before but the way she made my pussy flow was pro-
fessional. My legs were wide open, flesh ready to be devoured. It
was right there in her face, yet she felt like she wanted to play with
her food before she ate it. It's no wonder I called her "Bunny".
Although she teased the hell out of me, it caused my excitement to
rise. The promise of pleasure killed me. I felt my hips start to rotate
in an attempt to catch her mouth as it brushed past my snatch. The
second I couldn't take it anymore, I felt her whole tongue enve-
lope my wet, throbbing pussy. My back arched like a rainbow after
a spring rain. Her arms came up under my legs followed by her
hands gripping my thighs. For her to be so dainty, she had a bit of
strength to her. I opened my legs into a full split across her bed. If
this was her first time tasting glory, she was getting all of it. She
embraced it. There was no fear or hesitation while she dined at
my table. The moment I felt a finger slide inside me, I knew she
had been here before. My eyes rolled to the back of my head. She
beckoned my soul with every curl of her middle.
    The air began to become thick. The streetlights creeping
through the windows gave the room an Anytime, Anyplace vibe.
Orange and blue beams danced on the walls. I stared at the ceiling, bringing my focus directly to my clit being invited to climax.
While playing with my nipples, I closed my legs enough to wind
my hips. She moaned while she ate. The orgasm crowning within my walls began to emerge. I lifted myself up on my elbows to
watch her. She was fully engaged. Her tongue never tired. I told
her I was almost there. Where most men would have sped up after
hearing that, this deity of a woman nestled into my sweetness
and slowed her pace. She laid her entire tongue over my clit like
a blanket over a shivering body. I'd never had a harder orgasm
through oral sex. As I laid there panting, she came up to kiss me. I
held her face and exhaled through my nose while I kissed back. It
was the sweetest joy. Rolling over, we stared at each other briefly
and burst into satisfactory giggles. We laid there as two best friends
who just decided to give each other what we both needed. It didn't

become weird, nothing had to change - it was all good. Drifting off to sleep with our fingers entangled in each other's hair, everything just felt so right.

CHAPTER 5
The Odds

Mandisa

A week had passed, and Mozelle and I hadn't slept together since that night. It wasn't because of anything negative. We still talked every day like nothing happened, but our schedules just didn't allow us to connect like we wanted to. But that was going to change come later that night as our Cover Release Party was that night, and she was on the guest list.

The morning welcomed me with open arms. I was full of energy and ready to take over any challenge I was faced with that day. I was told I couldn't come into the office because I had to focus on making sure my energy was right for the party and my only job of the day was to show up, so I laid there briefly soaking in the sunlight. I thought about how my day needed to go. I had both an early afternoon hair and nail appointment but first...what to eat? Climbing my way out of bed, I put my robe on and went to the kitchen where I immediately started my coffee maker. The marble counters were gleaming and free of clutter. In the stillness of the kitchen, the appliances buzzed and hummed, and the coldness of the floor sent slight chills through me. I looked into the fridge to pull out the cream. The coffee's aroma began to fill the air. Grabbing my favorite mug, I poured the liquid energy into it and started to thank the Universe for the blessing of waking up. Breakfast was simple: 2 eggs, bacon, and toast. Nothing fancy but quite fulfilling.

After I ate, I sat on the couch for a bit of light reading. The 4-inch-thick textbook on how boss bitches operate consumed me for a little while. I was about halfway through and was intrigued by the author's point of view. As sitting there was very relaxing, I wanted to keep my stride going by getting a little yoga in as well, but I needed to let my breakfast settle before I started. I read another chapter and when I looked up, a half an hour had already passed, and I needed to get my mind right for this workout.

I wasn't good at it by my standards, but yoga had always helped in clearing my mind and getting me focused. The calmness and serenity of it was unmatched. I laid down my mat, sat in the middle of it and centered myself with meditation to start. Standing up, I began my warmup. I felt the stiffness in my limbs loosen. I allowed the energy around me to flow. By time I was done downward dogging, an hour had gone by, but it had only felt like 15 minutes. I was charged up and even more excited for the rest of the day to unfold.

As I put the mat back, I thought to myself how I needed to pick out my outfit for the party. Looking in my closet, I didn't see anything I particularly liked so I decided a trip to the Drive was in order after my hair and nail appointment. The Drive was a long strip full of clothing boutiques, shoe stores and coffee shops in the neighboring city. You could find some of the most elite shopping at The Drive: celebrities, politicians, beautiful, Black magazine owners, and the likes. After showering and getting dressed, I made my way down to the parking garage and headed out. It was such a gorgeous day, and I was so full of myself. My nail appointment was at noon and my hair at 1:45. Both went by smoothly and in a timely fashion. I was on my way to The Drive in no time.

In a city as packed as that one, it was a wonder I found parking so quickly. My truck was usually a park whisperer though so I guess I couldn't be too shocked. Stepping out, I took in the scenery. Fair skinned people were everywhere. Some shopping, some enjoying lunch at a bistro – this was where hippie meets boujie in the middle. The windows seemed invisible. They were so clean it was almost as if they weren't even there. All of the mannequins were dressed to kill. Every boutique had the season's hottest fashions on display. I didn't know which one I wanted to check out first. While I enjoyed walking through each shop, I hadn't quite found anything that grabbed my attention the way I needed it to. While walking through the street, I daydreamed about what the evening would hold regarding the release party. I was so excited about the entire event. After making my way to the other side of the boulevard, an outfit finally caught my eye. I walked in with anticipation.

The scent of freshly washed linens filled my nostrils. The lily-white walls and crystal chandeliers gave me a feeling of royalty. The hostess was most welcoming. She sprang towards me with a glass of champagne and offered her assistance.

"Hello! Welcome to Alice & France-Anna's! Can I help you," she asked.

"Yes, you can help me, actually. The ensemble in the window, I'd like to try it on please," I asked.

"Certainly! Follow me," she exclaimed. As she bopped along to the other side of the shop and I followed, I looked around to notice there were other women shopping and sipping as well. Most looked like housewives with nothing better to do with their days but spend money on clothes they would probably never wear.

The attendant showed me to the rack where my outfit hung. When I found my size, I went into a fitting room and tried it on. It fit perfectly. My breasts sat up beautifully in it and it hugged my ass like it had been ages since it saw one as round as mine. Coming out of the dressing room, I asked the young lady helping me if there was a pair of shoes that she would recommend to match the outfit. As it was a one-piece catsuit I would be wearing, the kicks could be nothing short of badass.

I made my way to the shoe section. As I walked up, there was another woman admiring a pair of stilettos. She was on the phone with whom I would assume was a girlfriend of hers. Her voice was incredibly loud and a little too familiar. As I made my way passed her, I glanced briefly and felt my heart stop. It was her - the woman who ruined my life. We caught eyes for what felt like ages until I looked away and browsed over shoes, trying to keep my composure. She was still flawless. Though aesthetically basic, she stood stout in her clear skin, long hair, and wide smile. It made me sick how flawless she was. Even the collar around her neck was…wait. Aziz collared her?! I know I didn't know all the ins and outs of the lifestyle, but I knew what a collar was and what it meant. To see she wore one as boldly as she did, created a wound deeper than the one I was already trying to heal. As I made the discovery, I heard a small snicker come from her chest as I assumed she recognized me too. My assumption turned into assurance as she vindictively started talking about Aziz.

"Naw girl, I'm not coming out tonight. My mother has the baby so me and Aziz could have some alone time and when I tell you he put it down last night?! He usually does but last night was something different. I woke up with a sore pussy like you wouldn't believe. Huh? No, he's at work right now and I'm out shopping. He gave me his credit card and told me to have fun. That's the least he could do after destroying my body the way he did…"

Everything in me wanted to snap. I could feel my body emitting its heat like a furnace in the dead of winter. My throat started to close, and my fists clenched. Hearing that Aziz still fucks her and fucks her the way he used to fuck me on top of that made me furious. Yet, instead of beating the life out of her, I simply turned away and took my outfit to the register. I practiced the paced breathing Mozelle taught me while wishing the cashier would hurry up. The second I signed my receipt, I snatched my bag and walked out. It took me a few paces up the boulevard and some deep breaths to calm down completely. She didn't deserve that type of time and energy from me. I made a conscious effort to let it go and not let it ruin the rest of my day. I had a release party to knock out and that's exactly what I was going to do.

When I got home, I immediately put on my Get Sexy playlist. The party was only a couple hours away and I needed every second to make sure I would be the flyest bitch in the building. After showering, putting lotion on and putting a cute bra and panty set on, I sat at my vanity mirror and admired myself. I felt glorious even in my bonnet. I said to myself my face had to be as flawless as my outfit. I decided since the catsuit was all black, the beat needed to be colorful. I looked at the shoes I purchased and mimicked their colors. When my face was fully beat, I walked over to the closet where my jumpsuit hung and traced my fingers over the fabric. I was about to go off at this club.

Looking at the clock, I realized I needed to put a little pep in my step. Trinnie had booked limousine services for us as well as the cover star and I only had 20 minutes until they arrived. I slipped my slim, thick body into my clothes and put my stilettos on. After I took my bonnet off and pin curls down, I gave myself a final look over. I was stunning. As I stood there gazing, I heard my doorbell ring. Opening the door, Mozelle stood there smiling, looking like somebody's artwork.

"Hey babe! You look great," she said. "The limo should be here in a few minutes so we should probably get downstairs."

"Ok! I just need to grab a clutch and then I'll be ready," I smiled. I tiptoed, hurriedly to the closet, grabbed a matching purse, filled it with necessary documents and lip gloss, following Bully out the door. We talked and giggled the entire elevator ride down.

Our driver was eagerly waiting and opened our door the second we stepped outside. We usually use the same limousine service for our events, so I immediately recognized our driver and was ecstatic to see him.

"Giovanni! Hey! What are you doing driving?!" I asked, greeting him with a kiss to the cheek.

"One of the perks of owning the place is being able to override assignments so you can escort one of your favorite clients to their big event. Wouldn't you say, Ms. Bloom?"

"You're so good to me, Gio," I smiled, dipping into the limo. Mozelle followed behind me with Giovanni closing the door behind her.

"You're loved everywhere you go. I'm here for it," she said.

"I don't know about that. I just treat people how I want to be treated and it usually works out for me," I laughed. Mozelle chuckled and pulled her hair back behind her ear. I stared at her shortly.

"You look beautiful tonight, Bully," I told her. She smiled from ear to ear looking back at me.

"Well thank you, Bunny. You're looking delicious yourself," she said as she playfully nudged me.

The limo ride was full of crazy stories and belly laughs that followed. Even Giovanni joined in the fun from up front. I was trying hard not to ruin my makeup with all the tears I was trying to stop from laughing so hard. When we pulled up to the club, there was a red carpet awaiting us. Giovanni came to open our door and my eyes immediately widened.

"What...the hell...did Trinnie do?" I mumbled to Mozelle. Seeing all the people outside like it was a major award show had her shocked as well.

"Chile, I have no clue..." she mumbled back. Nevertheless, we both smiled and waved like it was nothing. Walking up the red carpet, I heard news reporters and bloggers shouting my name.

"Mandisa! Mandisa! Are you ready for tonight?"

"Who are you wearing?"

"How are you going to top this month's issue?"

The flashing lights almost blinded me. All I could do was continue to smile. The attention was soon taken off of me as our cover star pulled up in her limousine. The crowd roared with excitement and cheers. As she stepped out of the car, we decided to wait for her so we could all walk in together. We had true hip hop royalty gracing our cover and she was just as magnificent in person as she was in our pages. She smiled as she walked up to us and held her arm out for me to grab. We walked into Rasa arm in arm while the fans swooned.

Rasa was absolutely gorgeous inside. High ceilings, 3 levels, black walls with purple, pink and green spotlights everywhere, a huge stage with our company logo dancing on a screen - it was impressive. The second we walked in, the DJ made a huge announcement of our arrival and our guests clapped, whistled, and made a lot of noise. After greeting and thanking everybody, the wait staff, clad in all black, immediately escorted us to a private VIP deck on the 3rd level where there were bottles upon bottles of champagne, a spread of fruits and cheeses, and a designated waiter serving our every need. There were magazine executives and other distinguished guests already in VIP waiting to greet us. They were so anxious to get a moment with our cover star.

Trinnie was so busy ripping and running trying to make sure that everything was perfect, that she hadn't had a second to stop and say hi. After the 3rd time of her running passed me, I forcefully snatched her up, said hi, kissed her on her cheek and let her go to continue to run the entire event. All I could do was laugh. The entire night was perfect. I hadn't seen Mozelle most of the night as she was likely on the lower-level dancing and mingling with people. My cover star was in the corner chatting with the mayor and a few other A-List people. I leaned over the balcony with my drink just absorbing the moment. A short while had gone by, and my thoughts were interrupted by Trinnie traipsing back towards me.

"There you are! I've been looking all over for you," she said. I looked at her a little weird as I was in the same spot all evening and I had to pull her aside to say hi, but I let it rock.

"I want you to meet the owner of this beautiful establishment," she continued. I chuckled as she adjusted her breasts before he reached us. I happily turned around to greet him but was immediately taken aback.

"Mandisa, I'd like you to meet..."

"Jeremiah..." I finished. I was like a deer caught in the headlights.

"Mandisa. Hello," he replied as he took my hand to kiss it.

"You two know each other?!" asked Trinnie. Jeremiah smiled, not taking his eyes off me.

"Yea, something like that," he said. Trinnie looked at us both staring at each other, smiled, and walked off.

"Alright then, I guess I'll leave you two to get reacquainted. I'll be down at the bar if you need me!"

Jeremiah was an old college beau. We were never officially a couple but secretly messed around all throughout school. We were both pretty popular on campus and hung around the same people, but no one suspected we were a thing and I liked it that way. Because my family-owned property in our college town, I was able to live off campus in one of the apartments which made it that much easier to creep. We didn't have to worry about anyone we knew seeing us. I remembered we had some good times. "Project Friday" was always the best. We were really close in school but after graduation, we ended up growing apart. I had no clue he ended up in this city.

"Mandisa Bloom. Look at you. Still fine, still shining. It's good to see you," he said, hugging me. He smelled like God on a rainy spring morning. I hugged him back and halfway didn't want to let him go.

"It's good to see you too, Remi! This is your place? It's beautiful. You must be really proud."

"Yea, I am. Business is good. If it keeps up, I may open a second location," he said.

"Wow, check you out. I'm impressed. But not really. You've always done amazing things." Our eyes remained locked. The slight grin on his face told me his thoughts were up to no good, but I paid it no mind.

After a few minutes of chatting, it was about time for me to reveal this month's cover. Jeremiah escorted both myself and my cover star down the stairs with us on his arms. Walking us to the stage, he stood beside me as I grabbed the mic. I could see he was all smiles. After a brief speech, I finally took the sheet down to reveal the cover. The crowd roared with approval. The wait staff brought copies of the issue out and handed them to each guest. Be-

62

cause of whom the artist was, we had to highlight her all through-out the magazine. She was overwhelmed with excitement.

"Mandisa, it's phenomenal! I'm in awe!" she exclaimed. Jeremiah walked up next to her, admiring it as well.

"I agree, Mandi. You did a superb job."

"Aw, thank you both! We worked really hard on it. It's really my staff who should get all the credit," I said. I pretended as if I didn't feel his hand on my shoulder - acted as if a chill didn't shoot down my spine the second his fingertips reached my shoulder. While I tried to brush it off, my cover star definitely took notice of it, looking directly at his hand then back at me with a smirk.

"Well, whoever is responsible deserves an immediate raise," she responded. I chuckled and slipped away from under Jeremiah's arm.

"I'll keep that in mind," I said. After she walked away, I turned to Jeremiah with a slight look of shock.

"What was that?" I asked.

"What? Was that awkward for you? Did I make you uncomfortable?"

"Yea, slightly."

"My apologies, Mandi. I didn't mean to. It just felt natural to me," he retorted. I looked him up and down then smiled. His eyes always got me.

"Whatever Remi. Don't be funny," I chuckled.

"What?! It did!" He paused briefly while looking at me. I wondered what was going through his mind.

"Can I get you anything?" he continued. I pulled my hair back behind my ear and softly exhaled.

"No, thank you. You and your staff took care of us well upstairs," I answered. His eyes beckoned me as if he didn't want to let me leave and I felt like I undressed him with mine. We stood there briefly fucking each other in our minds until Trinnie broke our gaze.

"Getting reacquainted, I see. Love that for you two. Uh, Mr. Grisham, do you mind if I borrow my boss for 2 seconds? We need her upstairs," she flirted. Jeremiah smiled.

"Absolutely. Deesie we'll catch up when this is over, yes?' he asked. I tried to keep it cool.

"Sure," I said with a smile as I walked off.

"Deesie, huh?" Trinnie, teased.

"Shut up. That's what he used to call me in college."

"College?!" she quietly exclaimed. "Oh, he's a throwback bae! Understood. Ya gonna buss it open for him again?"

"What?! Trinnie, calm down. I haven't seen him in years – since we graduated, in fact. I'm not about to just jump on him like a dog in heat," I snapped. Secretly, I had already pondered over the ways I'd toss this pussy at him. Even though my mind said no, my kitty begged for him in the panties I wore that night. He was still just as fine as he was when we were first dealing with each other. After all these years, he still gave me chills, yet I dismissed Trinnie's banter and followed her upstairs. After making it back, I was pleasantly surprised by a tribute from my staff with a congratulatory toast. It was the sweetest way to end such a stellar evening. They all did such an amazing job.

After everything started to die down and the crowd started exiting the building, I straggled behind not only to make sure everything was well with the venue but also to see if I could say goodbye to Jeremiah. He was nowhere in sight. I slowly walked towards the door as the bartenders, wait staff and cleanup crew broke down for the night. The lights were on, the chairs were resting upside down on the tables so the crew could mop and there I was sliding to the door in a snail-like manner. He was still nowhere to be found. The second I got to the door, I heard his voice and heaved a sigh of relief.

"Deesie! Deesie, wait!" he exclaimed as he chased after me. I turned around to see him unbuttoning his cuffs to loosen up for the night.

"Can I call you sometime? Maybe do dinner?"

"How are you going to have time for that, running a club and what not?"

"I own the place, babe. I have people that run the show when I have other obligations. It's not a problem to make time for you. So, can we exchange numbers?" The smile on my face could have melted the coldest of killers.

"I'd like that, Remi," I said. He handed me his phone for me to add my number. After pressing "Save", I handed it back with the most devious of grins.

"And you'd better use it, too," I winked. He called my

64

number immediately.

"Lock me in your phone. Make sure you answer when I call tomorrow," he smiled. I gave him one final look up and down and walked out of his club. I made sure to put every bit of sass in my step. When I got to the limo and shimmied to get in, I looked back and was excited to see Remi still in the door watching me. The butterflies in my stomach would not settle down. As Giovanni closed the door, my bliss was halted by two sets of eyes staring deep holes into me.

"What?" I asked.

"Aint no what! Bitch, you know what! Spill all of it!" Trinnie exclaimed.

"Spill what?!"

"The tea, bitch. The tea. Spill the tea. We saw you and Mr. Fine, Caramel as hell and Stacked all coochie crunch throughout the night. We want details!" Mozelle interjected. I giggled and shook my head.

"Jeremiah and I have known each other since college. We were sort of friends with benefits and after we graduated, we just went our separate ways. Nothing to write home about," I told them. They gave me the hardest side eye. I looked away because I couldn't face the interrogation.

"Uh uh, bitch. We need more than that. 'Cause the way ya'll two were googly eyed and goofy over each other all night, you would think ya'll have been in love for ages. Tell us everything," insisted Trinnie. She would never leave me alone about it until I told them the truth, so I caved in and told them what the deal was.

"Ok, that man right there?! Is a god. When we were in college we snuck around heavily, and nobody knew. I mean nobody. It was the sexiest shit to me. We'd be in a room full of our classmates, laughing and cutting up and the whole time we'd be sending messages to each other like 'I can't wait for you to touch the back of my walls' or 'that pussy was super wet this morning'. He had a key to my apartment and everything. He used to bust my ass," I confessed. Both Trinnie and Mozelle's jaws were dropped to the floor as I continued to give dirty details of my past with Remi. Mozelle then followed up with a series of important questions.

"So, do you think you'll fuck him again?"

I smiled bashfully and came clean about how I was feeling.

"To be honest, I cannot wait to let him destroy my guts again."

"YAAAAAAAAAS BITCH!!!" hollered Trinnie. Mo was enthused but also concerned given she knew about my needs.

"Well, what about the whole BDSM thing, babe? How are you going to introduce that into the mix? Are you going to introduce it?" she asked. I paused for a moment.

"I hadn't actually thought about that, but now that you mention it, I do wonder what that would be like. I think he has the demeanor to be a Dom but...I don't know. We always had bomb sex, but he was never the type to inflict the kind of pain I find myself enjoying. It's something I'd have to just...put out there. I'd probably have to teach him. But...we're speaking too fast. He hasn't even called me yet. Geez ya'll," I downplayed, shrugging my shoulders.

"Mmhm. This bitch is about to have that man putting her in all sorts of crazy positions. I love that for her," said Trinnie. We all erupted into hearty laughter and continued to crack jokes about it. As we dropped Trinnie off to her condo, she kissed both Mozelle and I on the cheek and stumbled up the stairs.

"She is so done," I laughed. Laying my head on Mo's shoulder, I exhaled deeply.

"Tonight was a great night, Bully," I said. She laid her head atop of mine.

"That it was, Bunny. That it was. You all pulled that off flawlessly, babe."

"Thank you," I paused. "What do you think will happen next?" I asked.

"Well babe, you're going to get home, get ready for bed, wake up the next morning, God willing and slay like you normally do. Everything in between that is the Universe tossing you cherries."

We both sat in silence, slipping into a light doze until Giovanni pulled up to our building. He opened the door and took my hand. I gave him a big smooch on his cheek and then the other for good measure.

"It was good to see you again, Gio. You know you don't have to wait until we need your services again to come check for

66

your girl, right?" Gio smiled and held my hand tight.

"Friends always, my lady," he responded as he kissed my hand. Helping Mozelle out of the limousine next, he closed the door and bid us farewell. She and I walked hand in hand to the door, through the lobby and into the elevator. She stared at me momentarily then kissed me softly.

"You deserve this happiness, Bunny," she said. I closed my eyes and kissed her back.

"Thank you, Bully. Are we good?"

"Always babe. Why wouldn't we be? You think because you're about to get some semi new dick, it's going to change our friendship? Girl bye." We both laughed and kissed each other one more time before the elevator stopped on her floor. Mozelle turned and looked back at me.

"I'll call you tomorrow boo. Get some rest."

"Yes ma'am," I obliged. I rested against the wall until I reached my floor. I had never been so relieved to see my door. I took my shoes off and walked down the carpeted trail. The sound of the lock turning was soothing. I undressed and showered quickly, collapsed on my bed, and drifted off to sleep over thoughts of Remi and what he used to do to me. I couldn't wait to hear from him.

CHAPTER 6
The Calm Before…

The next morning came with a beauty I couldn't describe. I had already told my entire staff that this day would be a late day for us all, so I was in no rush to get out of bed. I stared at my ceiling brushing stray hair out of my face. Turning my head to look at the time, I exhaled, happy that I still had plenty of time to be a hermit. Thoughts of Remi filled my head. I just couldn't get him out of my mind. It was incredibly good to see him again. Naturally he had changed since college. His shoulders were broader, his skin was still smooth and caramel colored. He let his beard grow full and thick and kept a low fade. When we hugged, his chest and arms felt solid and damn near burst out of his button down. I couldn't get over how well dressed he was and how good he smelled. I have a thing for men's accessories, so it was his necktie, diamond earrings and matching cufflinks for me. His smile was still as wide as it was back in school - eyes still deep brown like God hid all of His secrets behind them. That man was crafted from the deities.

My mind went back to those nights in my old apartment. He liked to call them "Project Friday". We were supposed to be studying for exams. We'd be in my bed and for a better portion of the evening, we would actually be studying. I'd be on my stomach in a bra and thong, and he'd be completely naked. That man never liked clothes. After a while, we'd both get restless - usually him before me. The one time that always stuck out to me was when he got tired of studying, he slowly climbed over top of me and began kissing the back of my neck. I could feel his dick, rock hard, pressing against the small of my back.

"Babe, we have exams tomorrow. We've gotta study," I whispered. He gently bit my neck then kissed it.

"I know baby, but you need to get this dick before we finish." He continued to grind on me and closed my ethics book without missing a beat. I smiled and allowed him to turn me on. We kept rubbers on the bed because we both knew what was eventually going down so when it was time, his hand didn't have to travel far to grab one. I remember the way my pussy juices saturated my pretty, blue lace thongs that were cradled in between my ass. Pulling them to the side after strapping up, Remi slid inside me slowly and methodically. That first thrust seemed very calculated as I recalled the chill that shot directly up my spine the second his

70

last inch of dick was covered in my pussy.

"Fuck, baby that pussy feel like it was waitin' for me," he said. I remember nodding my head and moaning so softly under him. I couldn't speak. Those first couple of strokes had me in bliss. I rolled my hips to keep from being a lazy fuck and it amused him a little bit.

"Look at you, throwin' it back on me. Give it to me then. C'mon." Remi was so good at putting a battery pack in my back. The more he said, 'give it to me', the harder my hips rocked underneath him. He loved it. Pulling out to turn me over on my back, Jeremiah pulled the soaking wet thongs from off me and got right back in it. I screamed loud. It felt like the sounds I made, in turn put a battery pack in his back because the louder I got, the harder he went.

"Yeeea baby, I got in there good just now, huh?" he grinned.

"Ah shit! Remi it's so b...bi..."

"Bi...bi...BIG. Yea baby I know. Big dick shit. Now gimme all of that pussy," he boasted. And I gave it to him too. Back then, I was a slim, lil thing but I knew how to take his dick fairly well. This particular time though, I was feeling myself a little too hard. While on my back, I put my right leg over his shoulder and his palm was pressing my left thigh to keep in on the bed. Slightly shifting on my left side, I began to rock my hips again to allow my pussy to meet and greet his staff with ease.

"Mmmmm Remi, that's it right there. Don't stop," I moaned.

"Stop for what? This pussy is amazing. I'ma keep fuckin' so you can keep cumming. Cum for me," he demanded. It was something about that position that caused him to hit my spot every single time. It started to get so good. I lifted up and supported myself with my elbows and pounded my body against his. Remi loved it.

"Yeeea, that's what I came here for. Fuck on me then. Fuck on me til you cum. Get that nut for yourself. Here, let me give you more dick to help you," he said as he pushed as deep as it would allow him. He held it there for a couple of seconds, went back to stroking before holding it there again. He fucked in that pattern a few more times. I felt an orgasm building up. I screamed and moaned until I creamed all over his dick. The evil grin on his face was priceless as he kept stroking. He took it out, attempting to tease me but I was too turned up, so I chased him for it.

"Put it back, baby put it back!! I wanna cum again!" I yelled. Remi always got a kick out of me chasing his dick, but he'd always let me catch it, teasing me in the process of putting it back in.

"Here! Wit' ya greedy ass! You just came hard. How many more times you wanna cum?" he asked, knowing good and damn well he wasn't about to stop. I was almost to the point of tears, it felt so good.

After a second orgasm, he took it out again, put my legs all the way back and licked from ass all the way up to my clit, sucking a 3rd one out damn near right after the one prior. Once I was down off that climax, he continued to eat me until I squirmed and begged him to stop. He kept a goatee back then and when he finally came up for air, it was dripping wet. I pulled him up by his ears and kissed him deeply, getting my entire face wet too. While kissing, he slid back inside me and went back to destroying my walls.

My moans were stifled by his kiss but when he pressed on my cervix, I severed our connection and let out the loudest scream. He bit down on my neck and grunted like a beast. I felt him throbbing. After easing up on me, I smiled and chuckled softly.

"Mmm. That must've been that nut," I teased. Still on top of me with a piece of my neck still between his teeth, he nodded, trying to catch his breath. We both laughed as he pulled out and let go of my neck. After cleaning up, we went right back to studying until we both fell asleep.

I think why that particular time stood out to me was because of the enormous hickey he left on my neck and everybody asking about it the next day in class, including him. I wore that passion mark with pride. It tickled me to see him a part of the banter from our classmates knowing I got it from him digging deep in my guts. Our relationship was so weird in college, but I was there for it. Just as I smiled thinking about it all, a text notification came through. It was from Remi:

"Rise and shine, sleepy head."

The smile on my face could have bested the sun. It was the cutest text to me. My cheeks started to hurt as I responded...

Remi

I thought about Mandisa all night. In college, we were the best of friends - thick as thieves. More like thick as her thighs now because goddamn. She was always sexy as hell but seeing her now had my dick hard since she left my club the night before. I didn't think I would ever see her again, let alone run into her in my establishment. She never left my thoughts and it had been years since we graduated. Damn, it was good to see her. My reminiscing was disrupted by my ex turned over, still asleep.

Her naked body lay warm next to me, but it still felt ice cold in my bed. We had broken up a couple of months prior, but she showed up to my house the same night of Mandisa's party. It was 2 in the morning and all I hear is my doorbell ringing. When I opened the door, my ex stood there sobbing and saying she missed me. She was clearly drunk, stumbling into my arms, begging for a second chance to make things right. Her car was parked in my driveway on a slant so there was no way I could put her out and let her drive off. I brought her inside and told her to lay down on the couch. When I went upstairs to shower and lay down, I came out and found her in my bed with no clothes on.

"Jeremiah, fuck me. You know you miss this," she slurred as she scooted closer to the edge of the bed.

"I don't think that would be wise, Leilani," I said.

"What's the matter? Gone soft on me?" She reached for my towel and tried to unfold it from around me. I moved her hands and held them at the wrists.

"You're drunk. I can smell the alcohol all over you. I'm not setting myself up like that," I told her. While trying to keep her off me, I grabbed the remote that controlled my cameras in the room for precautionary reasons and started recording. I had no intentions of fucking that girl and with the way we split, I wouldn't put anything passed her.

"You need to lay down and go to sleep," I continued. I grabbed my robe, covered her in it and led her to the guest room. She protested the entire time.

"Jeremiah why are you being like this?! You know you

73

want me back!" she cried. I sat her on the bed and walked away.

"Go to sleep, Leilani!" I urged. I went back to my room, put some pajama pants on and got in my bed.

I couldn't get Mandisa out of my head. Memories of how we used to be consumed me until I fell asleep. When I woke up, Leilani was next to me. Although I was disgusted, I let her sleep, laying there thinking about Deesie, so I sat up on the side of the bed and decided to text her.

"Rise and shine, sleepy head." That had to have sounded so lame to her but her near immediate response made me smile.

"It's too early for your shit. I just left your club like 10 minutes ago" she said. It was funny to see she was still dramatic. While I was texting back, Leilani started to wake up from the dead and I was ready to put her out.

"You need to go home and not come back here," I scolded. She got up silently and ashamed as she picked her clothes up off the floor. When she got dressed, she headed to the door.

"I'm sorry," she said. I didn't respond. I simply continued to stare at my phone waiting for Mandisa to respond to my last text. Leilani stood in the doorway hoping I would say something, however, when I didn't, she walked out. I heard her car door slam and her engine start. When I felt confident that she was off my property, I laid back down. Another text came through that got me hype.

"Why don't you just call me so we can talk, and I can still keep my eyes closed." Mandisa was always a brat, but it was cute to me because she wouldn't hurt a fly. I played her little game and called her phone. Her voice was low and slightly raspy just how I remembered it being in the mornings we would wake up next to each other.

"Hey Remi," she muttered happily. Hearing the pet name only she called me was soothing.

"Wassup lady. How we feelin' this morning? You good from last night?"

"Yea, I'm ok. A little bit of a headache but other than that I'm fine. How are you?"

"I'm gettin' there. Just had to shuffle my ex's drunk ass on up outta here."

74

"Geez, how'd that go?"

"She showed up here drunk trying to sleep with me, crying and begging me to come back"

"I can believe that. You always had a power over women"

"What do you mean?! I don't do much,"

"Yeah ok. You must have forgotten who you're talking to," she snipped. She and I never had a problem with discussing our relationships. At one point in school, I had a girlfriend, and she had a man and it never bothered us. We would still creep around so me telling her I just had to put my ex out was of no consequence. I laughed at her comment.

"Whatever, Deesie. Wassup with you though? I know you got a man chasin' after you." She hesitated.

"Naw. My ex and I broke up a few months ago." I wasted no time after I heard that.

"Wow. That's fucked up. Sooo...see you later then?"

"Damn!" she bellowed with laughter. "Later, what time?" I hate to admit this but hearing that made me feel a rush like I was on a decline of a high ass roller coaster. I told her to be ready by 7 and I'll have my driver pick her up. She agreed and we said our goodbyes. I heaved a sigh and looked around. What in the world was I going to plan for this woman? I had always been good at planning last minute outings and spur of the moment dates, but Mandisa wasn't the average woman that an average date would appease. She deserved the red carpet rolled out and I wanted to give it to her. I mulled over some ideas then checked the weather. I knew just the thing that would have her melting in my hands.

Mandisa

After getting off the phone with Remi, I scratched my head
and wondered what I was about to be getting myself into. I was excited to be seeing him again, but it had been a few years since we
last saw each other. Things have changed. We've gotten older, I've
gained weight, I've gained more experience sexually – I was not
the woman he once knew. When I thought about those things, I felt
confidence build up. A bitch was about to bust Remi's ass sooner
or later!

I called Trinnie and told her to do a blast call telling the
staff I had decided to give us all a personal day. We had just pulled
off one of the hottest issues of the season because of the hard work
my employees put in so we could afford an office wide emergency
day off. After all, I was getting ready to link up with my secret college sweetheart. I wanted to take the day to myself. I told Trinnie
what was up, and she was so thrilled.

"Bitch, I want every single detail when it's over!" she
gasped. I laughed hysterically after her.

"Trinnie, I'm not fucking him tonight...I don't think. We're
just linking up to catch up."

"Well go get waxed just in case. In fact, add Mo to this call.
Spa day, bitch. We need to get you dick ready." Tears began to roll
down my face from laughing so hard as I added Mo to the call. She
answered half asleep.

"What do you bitches want? Didn't we just leave the club
together?" she answered, groaning.

"Mo!! Mandi has a date with Mr. Fine, Caramel as hell and
Stacked tonight!" yelled Trinnie. If I knew Mozelle, she quickly
popped her head up before saying:

"Forreal? Oh, nah spa day, hoe. You need your cat
snatched," she taunted.

"Bully!" I shouted.

"What?!" she argued. "I just had my face in it last week!
You do!" she finished. You could hear Trinnie fall off the bed, dying laughing. My face turned up in disgust.

"I can't stand you bitches," I retorted as I looked in my

panties realizing they were right.

"I'll book the appointments! Yoni steam too, yes?" asked Mo.

"Yea and see if they have rhinestones they could put on it!"

"Trinnie, one thing at a time. We gotta knock the cobwebs off the bitch first"

"You right, Mo, you right. Book it!"

It upset me slightly that these hoes were having an entire conversation about my vagina like I wasn't there, but their laughter lightened the whole argument, and I began to chuckle with them. Trinnie said she would be here in half an hour to give us time to get ready. I showered, put on a cute fit and grabbed a banana on the way out the door.

We could hear Trinnie coming from around the corner, the way she blasted her music. Our heads started bobbing as we heard 90's classics getting louder until she approached. We hopped in her truck and sped off with the doors barely closed. I rode shotgun and Mo sat comfortably in the back texting. Trinnie broke out in hives anytime she had to drive under 60 miles per hour, so she immediately became irritated with the traffic on my avenue.

"Ya'll had to live on the busiest street in the city?! Damn!" she hollered while beating up her steering wheel. Mozelle and I chuckled and shook our heads. Trinnie was about to give us all whiplash the way she turned down the next side street just to avoid the pileup. I was excited to go get my kitty pretty, but I didn't want to die behind it. That woman drove like a maniac.

We entered the spa as true divas. Mozelle told the attendant to put everything on her account and switched straight to the back. Trinnie and I followed as our hostesses came to greet us. I was impressed at how quickly we were received. The place was gorgeous: rose gold and ivory tile on the walls in the corridor, the floors were hardwood and loud as our heels clicked into them. There were portraits of Black women with cucumbers over their eyes and seaweed masks covering their facial skin. The music was low and tranquil. We were met by our specialists who suggested we get our yoni steams done first as it would make for an easier removal during our waxing then led us to the locker room to change. I had never done a yoni steam before, so it was all brand new to me.

We walked into the steam room, and it was one of the sexiest rooms I had ever seen. Our specialist told us that Yoni steaming was a ritual in their establishment, so the ambiance had to be right: a dimly lit space, Solfeggio frequencies playing, stones and crystals around each pot which were sitting on thrones. There were attendants preparing our steaming pots. The scent of the herbs and flowers filled the air causing my eyes to slowly close and my lips to form a slight smile. When the pots were ready, each attendant helped us up the two stairs that led to the yoni thrones. I followed Mo and Trinnie's lead as they have done this before. I sat over the pot and jumped at the sensation I felt.

"Oh my," I blurted out. The girls chuckled as they were fully aware I had no idea what I was doing. After getting comfortable, we all breathed deeply. We had the room to ourselves, so we were able to discuss recent turns of events freely. Mozelle told us of her considering buying a building for her practice, Trinnie gave us a rundown of her latest sex-capade with bouncer bae and how he's talking about marriage, and I decided to tell them about my little encounter the day before.

"I bumped into Aziz's baby mother yesterday." The room fell silent for a split second as Trinnie and Mo looked at each other then back at me.

"Bitch, where?!" whispered Trinnie, trying not to yell.

"On the Drive. She was in one of the boutiques I stopped in"

"What was *that* like?"

"Gut wrenching. She was on the phone with someone talking about what Aziz did to her and how he gave her his credit card to go shopping with...I just bought my outfit and left."

"You should have clipped the bitch," scoffed Mo.

"That wouldn't have solved anything," I said.

"Yeah, but I'm sure you would have at least felt better," she replied. We all laughed at the thought. I adjusted the pillow soft, black robe I wore to make sure my breasts were still covered and rested my head back on the throne. Though I tried to make it look like I was ok, inside I was sick. Seeing her again brought about a sadness I couldn't put into words. My self-esteem definitely took a hit because the woman was stunning. She looked more like someone Aziz should be with than I did. I was a little girl compared to her. She was taller, built a little heftier - she just looked all around better suited to stand next to him. Self-doubt penetrated my thoughts harder than a dick getting pussy for the first time. Who was I to Aziz? Why did he waste my time if he was going to cheat? Why wasn't my love and submission enough? Questions I'd never get answers to circulated through my mind while the piping hot steam wafted fragrant fumes over my honeywell permeating my skin ever so gently. After a few minutes of stillness, I felt myself begin to relax. I kept my eyes closed and began to take counted breaths. The herbs in the water were doing their job. Fuck Aziz and his perfect baby mama.

The treatment lasted about a half an hour. Our attendants handed us towels and emptied our bowls before escorting us to the hallway. We were met by 3 estheticians who were waiting to start our waxes. Parting ways into separate rooms, I gave the girls a high 5 and stepped into mine. I disrobed and climbed up onto the waxing table. It'd been a few months since I last had a wax, so I mentally prepared myself for pain. My waxing specialist was friendly and didn't make me feel bad about the forest she had the responsibility of chopping down. We chatted about little nothings like weekend plans and recent celebrity news as she ripped the hair from each follicle.

She spread the first strip down as I stared at the ceiling while she did her thing with a popsicle stick. Asking me what I did for a living, I could tell she was trying to distract me from the pain she was about to inflict and before I could get out the words "Editor in Chief", she snatched the first strip and applied pressure to quickly alleviate the sting. I winced and grunted with each yank of wax. Fortunately, the process was quick and the discomfort, short-lived. I ran my hand across my skin and loved the smooth-ness, looking at myself in the mirror as my specialist sanitized her station. It was a beautiful sight - my pussy was so clean; I didn't know what to do with myself. I could even see my piercing again, I thought. I put my robe back on and headed to the main hall to wait for the other two to finish getting waxed.

Mozelle came out of her room almost simultaneously. You could hear Trinnie popping off in a joyous way in her room. As she walked out, she opened her robe and flashed everybody to show us her freshly snatched cat.

"Look at this thang!! Ain't she pretty?! Pretty Kitty!

79

Aooow!" she danced. Mozelle's jaw was on the floor when I looked at her while the rest of the ladies waiting in the hall just laughed and cheered her on. Mo' yanked her by her arm and pulled her all the way to the locker room.

"You're so embarrassing!" she said in a hushed but assertive tone.

"You mad? Had a couple hairs that wouldn't budge? It's ok. I can pluck them when we get back to ya'll place if you want," Trinnie teased. I laughed from my belly watching Mo's face slowly relax until a chuckle came through her lips. No one could ever stay mad at Trinnie as she would never allow it. You just couldn't help but to love her and laugh at her antics. Fully dressed, feet in heels, we grabbed our bags and headed to the front desk to get Mo's card, giggling the whole way.

"So, what's the plan for tonight?" asked Mo as we stepped out into the parking lot.

"I'm not sure," I answered. "He just said be ready by 7 and his driver will pick me up."

"His driver?" Trinnie asked, noticeably impressed. "Bitch, give him all of the pussy tonight."

"All of it. Every corner. Every pocket. Each drop of pussy butter...all of it," added Mo. The look I gave the both of them was priceless.

"Ya'll, I'm not even on it like that. We're going to catch up. That's it." I lied. They both could see right through me.

"Bitch, you just got a whole forest yanked out of your vagina. Please stop with the bullshit," chimed Trinnie. I could always count on those two to keep me in check. We hopped into the car, driving off into the afternoon sun with bald pussies and joy in our hearts.

While we cruised, I sat shotgun thinking about what it was going to be like. I still had it in my head that I was absolutely going to put it all the way on him that night. There was no way he'd be able to keep up with the beast I've become sexually. I fantasized about how it would all go down - how I would show my confidence and take him whole. My thoughts went from how I would ride and what I would say to how hard I would throw it back until they were interrupted by my cell phone ringing. It was Remi. I answered with such enthusiasm. Before I could get a word in edgewise, Trinnie grabbed my phone.

"Hey handsome! Make sure you fuck my girl good tonight, ok? We got the cobwebs knocked off of it really good so you should be able to find it well enough," she clowned. I snatched the phone from her as hard as I could and put it to my ear to hear him laughing.

"Oh my god! I'm so sorry! We don't take her out much, so she really doesn't know how to act!" I scoffed, popping Trinnie with the back of my hand. She stuck her tongue out, snickered, and kept driving. Remi's laughter assured me that I didn't have to be ashamed of my wild comrade.

"Nah, it's all good, baby. That was pretty funny. You all set for tonight?" he asked.

"Yeah, for the most part. Just need to figure out what to wear," I answered.

"You don't have to go crazy. It'll just be me and you."

"Oh ok. I think I can figure it out from here, then,"

"That's what I like to hear. Well, alright then. I'll see you a little later."

"See you later, boo," I said with a smile I'm sure he could see from where he was. When I came back down from a moment of daydreams, I popped Trinnie again.

"Why would you get on my phone and say that?!" I snapped.

"Now you know how I felt," retorted Mo from the back seat.

"Oh, shut up! I did you a favor," Trinnie cackled. Lord knows I could have slapped her in that moment but internally, I thanked her. It almost solidified that I was getting some that night. As I went back to daydreaming, a text message from Remi came through:

"Pack a bag"

There was nothing that could hide the smile that grew on my face nor that could stop my body from reacting the way it did. My walls began to pulsate, and my palms became sweaty. I had to keep fidgeting in my seat because the feeling of an involuntary orgasm became inevitable. Remi always had that effect on me. Fortunate enough to get the feeling to subside, I jumped out of Trinnie's truck with haste when she pulled up to the front. I blew her a kiss, leaving Mo still struggling to get out of her seatbelt.

When I got up to my apartment, I slammed the door and stood there catching my breath thinking about what I needed to pack. I grabbed one of my travel bags and immediately stuffed it with the necessities. Once done, I looked through my clothes and picked out a cute blue cardigan and light blue jeans. I made sure to pull out a matching bra and thong set as I wanted to be a piece of eye candy the whole way through.

I still hadn't responded to his text yet. I guess the excitement from even getting it overwhelmed me. I did want to acknowledge it and not just leave him on "read" but I didn't want to send a regular "ok" as a response either. I thought about what I wanted to get out of the evening. Remi and I always had amazing sex but with everything I indulged in after we parted ways post college, I wondered how we could incorporate it into what we were about to do. There were several things I knew: I was going to fuck him, it wasn't going to be a one-night thing and I needed to make sure I got my desires met. I sat down on my bed, thought for a second and finally responded to his text:

"Not a problem but I need you to research these things before 7 o'clock: BDSM, submissive, safe words and aftercare. If you're cool with what you discover then awesome. But if you aren't, let me know before I get there, please."

It was read almost instantly but it took him a little time to respond. I sat there with my thoughts for a moment wondering if he thought I was crazy after he looked at my texts. The second I got up; I heard my phone go off. I was relieved to see he responded but worried about what the response would be. As I read, I breathed a sigh of relief:

"Oh, that's what you like now? I got it."

Excellent. I knew Remi had me covered because there had never been anything I asked him for or asked him to do that he could not accomplish in the past. Without a care in the world, I set my alarm and laid down for a quick nap, drifting off to sleep with thoughts of Remi's body over mine.

Remi

When Mandisa responded to my text telling her to pack a bag, I did not anticipate her response. I knew she would be with it, but I was not expecting to do homework beforehand. Since it was her requesting this from me, I did what she asked and researched BDSM, submissive, safe words and aftercare. I had to admit that I didn't know the first thing about any of it but if it pleased Mandi, I'd be excited to learn. Even in college I liked to make sure she was good before I got mine. Before we ever started fuckin' around and I was "just a friend", she told me she had never had an orgasm through penetration before. Whatever fuckboy she was dealing with didn't what he was doing, and it caused her to believe something was wrong with her. When I got my hands on her, not only was she orgasming with my dick deep inside her, but she was having multiples. The first time she came through penetration, she had no clue what was happening and cried but begged me to do it again – and I did over and over. I knew her body better than she knew it. I made it do things Mandisa never knew it could do. It had her aching to please me. Now that I think about it, that BDSM stuff wasn't too far-fetched from what we had in school. She was always so eager to please me. I mean she really knew how to put it on for me. She spoke my language better than any woman I have ever been with and just as she was so open to me, my nostrils were flared for her. My lust and infatuation with her were insane and it fueled my desire to learn everything I could about pleasing her.

I read up on the basics just to get familiar with what she was talking about. I assumed that based off of her demeanor, she liked to be in a submissive state. Again, she was always so willing to please and was constantly up under me when we were together so reading about what a sub/Dom dynamic was made sense. I always made the decisions in what we had. Yea, we were keeping our thing a secret, but we were absolutely in a relationship, and I ran the show. Diving further into research, it was an interesting read regarding BDSM as I never thought that Black people were into this kind of thing. At first glance, it would be like 'oh nah that's White people shit' but here, I have this beautiful, redbone goddess inadvertently telling me she likes to be tied up and spanked until she needs a safe word and aftercare. I was with the shits but damn Mandi...what were you about to get me into?! The more I read, the more I came to understand that that's not what BDSM is all about. It was fascinating to me that it is an actual way of everyday life for people. Ok Deesie. That's what you into? Cool. I got it.

I made a quick phone call to a homegirl of mine who I knew sold adult novelties and had her swing by the house. She threw a launch party at the club once, so I knew she had what I was looking for. Shorty wasted no time getting there either. Withing 20 minutes of our call, she was at the door with an entire trunk of shit I could pick from. She seemed like the type that would know more about the subject at hand so as she unloaded items, I told her what I was looking to do, and she pulled out what she thought suited my needs best. Handcuffs, blindfold, a strap with a ball in the middle, suede pom poms and long stick with jeweled out handle on one end and leather at the other.

"Breh, what the fuck is this?" I asked, examining the long toy. She laughed as she was plugging something into the wall.

"It's a horse crop, sir"

"And what do you do with it?"

"You spank bitches with it, sir. But that's fairy tale stuff compared to what I'm about to show you, she answered, turning on a contraption that lit up and lightly buzzed when she turned the dial at the bottom of it.

"What the fuck is...AH!!!" I screamed jerking my arm back as a small jolt of static electricity sizzled on my arm. Home-girl couldn't stop laughing.

"It's a violet wand. It uses electricity to stimulate the body. I had it on a medium setting so you could feel it but there are much milder settings on it that offer a lighter sensation on the skin if you're just starting out," she explained. I rubbed my arm with exaggeration.

"Leave all of it and tell me what I owe you," I said. She drafted an invoice, named her price, and I handed it to her in cash. As she packed up her trunk and left, I examined everything I purchased. Looking at my receipt, I found out the suede pom poms were not actually pom poms at all but floggers. While I was fully prepared to be a cheerleader that night, I felt like they would be better purposed tapping on Mandisa's pretty ass. I took everything upstairs, displayed it on the bed and read up a little bit more on safe words and aftercare.

The closer it became to 7 o'clock, I felt like I had done enough research of everything she needed me to, to at least be able to have a conversation about it over dinner. My chef was downstairs in my kitchen preparing dinner for us and the butler prepared the deck for dinner before he retired for the evening. I showered, shaved, and laid in bed with nothing on but a towel until I heard my driver pull up with Mandisa in tow.

CHAPTER 7
...the Storm

Mandisa

Remi's driver pulled up to a huge, secluded house in the suburbs. Surrounded by trees with a long driveway leading to what seemed like an all-glass house, my eyes became as wide as my legs were about to be. He definitely made out well for himself. His driver carried my bag into the house as I meekly followed, looking up at the high ceilings - a bit intimidated to say the least. I was interrupted by a chef who graciously greeted me as he was coming into the house from an outside patio.

"Good evening, Miss," he greeted. "Mr. Grisham will be down shortly. Dinner is waiting for you on the terrace." The wrinkles and moles on his face told me that he'd been a chef for some years and what I was about to feast on would be amazing. His West Indian accent further told me that Remi knew what he was doing hiring him as a chef, considering Caribbean cuisine is a favorite of mine.

As the chef gathered his tools and put them in the kitchen drawers before leaving, I took in the space a little more, waiting for Remi to come down. It was fully open. Some rooms seemed to flow into others effortlessly. Amidst the glass walls, there was a column of white-painted bricks that gave way to a fireplace. While the weather didn't quite call for it at the time, it was a beautiful addition to the home. The furniture was modern and chic, there was art everywhere and when I turned around to see behind me, there was a huge fish tank built into one of the walls that led to an entirely different section of the house. After a few minutes of soaking it all in, Remi came downstairs.

"Deesie, you made it," he greeted. I turned around to acknowledge him and my eyes damn near popped out of my head. He was coming down the stairs completely naked, dick just swinging as he got lower. I paused and then burst into laughter as that has always been what Remi does. If I had to bet, he was a nudist in one of his past lives because I swear, he never liked to wear clothes in the house back in school either. We hugged and kissed each other's cheek. He snatched a black robe that laid across the couch and I took notice of a second one positioned next to it. As he tied his, he

88

gathered the other one and handed it to me.

"Get comfortable. There's a bathroom right there if you'd prefer. I'll be outside," he commanded. The robe he handed me was shorter than his. Undoubtedly a woman's robe, I gave him a short-lived side-eye and went to change. I kept my bra and thong on as I remained on a mission to give him that work. Giving myself a brief look over, I was pleased at what I saw. The robe sat perfectly below the cusp of my thighs and ass, not one hint of ash anywhere, and my face was beat with makeup that I was praying would get ruined later in the evening. Once I gave myself the stamp of approval, I exhaled and left the bathroom fully confident that Remi's soul was going to be tucked away neatly in my bra by the end of the night.

I stepped out onto the patio to feel a gentle breeze sweep my face. The sun had not quite set yet, but she was almost ready to say goodnight to us both. Remi looked me up and down as I sat in the seat reserved for me. Though his economic status had changed, his vernacular was still in the hood.

"Wassup?!" he grinned.

"Still silly, I see. This is your home?! It's beautiful!"

"Yeah, I do a lil' something here and there. What's up with you? How's life, Ms. Editor in Chief?" he inquired, pouring me a glass of wine. I noticed the bottle and began to melt as it was my favorite type of vino.

"Remi, you remembered," I approved. He was briefly confused until he noticed me looking at the bottle.

"Huh? Oh! What'chu mean?! Of course, I did. Riesling, right? It's all you drank in school. I hope you like this brand. I had my assistant pick it out when I had her purchase your robe today. Do you like it?" he asked. I took a sip and smiled.

"Yes. She picked out a good one."

"No, I meant the robe," he said with a splash of assertiveness.

"Oh! Yes, this is lovely too," I responded. He then lifted our plate covers to reveal a gorgeously prepared Chilean sea bass with mixed bell peppers and cilantro lime rice. I was completely beside myself.

Over dinner, we caught up on life and laughed at old memories from college. The entire time, I felt the feelings I had

89

for him back then creep up on me. This time however, I let them grow freely. Back in school I tried hard to suppress them because I enjoyed the anonymity of it all but in this present juncture, there was nobody to hide from. Nothing had changed about our vibe. The only thing that had changed was I was a little more seasoned sexually and probably better than him - or so I thought. The amazing food was demolished, yet we sat on the terrace until the bottle of Riesling was emptied. The conversation then took a slight turn.

"So, tell me about this lifestyle you call yourself into now," Remi said. I responded with the most devilish grin on my face and told him how I had discovered a need in me to be controlled. I explained to him what submission looks like for me and he absorbed as much information as he could. He was particularly intrigued about the part where I told him I like pain and in which way I like it.

"So, do you think you'll need a...what'd you call it? A safe word with me?" he asked. I knew he still had no clue what he was about to get into, so I simply smiled and told him yes, expounding on what it was.

"Safe words are essential and should be put into place in any dynamic. It's a boundary that should be respected if invoked. I like it rough, and you've always liked to give me what I want and pursuant to that, things may get out of hand. So yes. A safe word is required. Mine is Neruda,' I told him. He made a face that said he was thoroughly impressed with my confidence. What I didn't tell him was that my safe word was given to me by my ex. It was just so beautiful to me and when I was told where it derived from, it made it that much more beautiful.

"Neruda," he repeated. Pausing briefly to process it all, he looked at me with determination in his eyes and continued.

"...and so, you need me to dominate you. What does that look like to you?" he asked. The fact that he was even curious about everything I dumped in his lap turned me on even more. I described to him the things that I needed to be controlled by another human being.

"Remi, I need you to control everything around me when I'm with you. I don't want to think, I don't want to breathe, I don't want to function without your permission. I need every orgasm, every heavy breath I take, every convulsion to be because you allowed it." I explained. He looked very absorbed in what I was saying.

"Understood. Aftercare. Explain that to me," he said. I loved his attentiveness while I spoke. He didn't take his eyes off me once while I spelled out what that meant.

"Aftercare is what needs to happen after a scene in order to bring your submissive down safely from the high she is experiencing. There are a bunch of hormones and chemicals that mix to put a person into what's called sub-space. It's a euphoric space that we experience during play..." I explained. I took everything Aziz taught me and presented it to him as if I'd known all along what I was talking about.

"And how can I bring you down safely?" he asked. I had to pause and think about my next response. Not because I didn't know the answer but because thinking about it stirred up feelings and sensations that I had no control over, and I had to make sure I explained it with clarity.

"I need to be held - soft, low tones in my ear," I whispered. My eyes began to slowly close as flashbacks of nights with Aziz came to mind. His scenes were always what I needed them to be and for a split second, I became lost. As I bit my bottom lip, Remi sensed I was drifting.

"Where are you right now?" he asked. His voice sounded almost distant as I was mentally traveling back to Aziz's bed. I feared I would never be able to let go of him. He still had so much power over me, but I was doing a disservice to Remi and to myself by staying tied to him. I heard Remi call to me again.

"Mandisa. Come back to me," he beckoned. In a daze, I watched him get up from the table and hold his hand out for me to take. A vision of my first night as Aziz's submissive surfaced. I turned my head to try to banish the thought from my mind. I placed my hand in it, uncrossing my legs to raise up. His hand, unbeknownst to him, provided temporary relief for the massive load of anxiety that rested on my chest. Before I got up, I was bewildered as I came back to full consciousness, looking into his eyes and finding my soul already there. We locked gazes as his free hand swept my hair behind my ear.

"There you are," he smiled. As I stood, a gush of fluid came down so hard, I swore my period had just started. I gasped softly, looked at Remi with fear in my face, then looked down as I hesitated to move. Every thought relevant to the moment crossed my mind: this shit would happen right now. But it's early. It's not due for another week! I'm not prepared at all!

Remi paused to observe me. When he realized what I thought was happening, I looked up to see a slight grin on his face as he stepped closer towards me, still hand in hand. He looked me fully in the eye and with the same hand that brushed my face, coasted it down my torso, slipped his fingers through my robe and into my thongs to see what was up. When he felt the overflow of liquid, a look of shock came over his face as he pulled them out to see what was coating them. I closed my eyes in horror, thinking the worst.

"Let me fuckin' find out," he said in a calm yet eager tone. I opened my eyes to see him admiring a healthy amount of pussy juice running down his fingers. Watching him put them in his mouth directly after, comforted me. I was so relieved. I would have been pissed off had Mother Nature played me like that. But to my advantage, his reaction to it gave me fuel to keep believing I was going to bust his entire ass and hold the key to his manhood afterwards. I kissed him, tasting my sweetness on his lips. Taking his face in my hands, my confidence followed me all the way to my doom.

Remi led me back into the house and up a flight of stairs. The hallways were dimly lit by candlelight - the walls, a dark gray, dressed in beautiful artwork. A plush, white carpet hugged my bare feet. As we got closer to his bedroom, the sound of tantric music twirled in my ear. Approaching the door, he pushed it fully open and allowed me to walk through first. He had candles everywhere. The smell of grapefruit filled the air - it was my favorite scent. I turned to look at him with the biggest smile on my face.

His room was huge with wall-to-wall carpet similar to the one in the hallway. There was what I dubbed a double king size bed in the middle room with a headboard crafted to the gods. As we got closer to the bed, I gasped with excitement when I saw the delicious spread of toys and tools laid out. I stood at the foot in awe. There were paddles, blindfolds, chains, handcuffs, feathers, vibrators, a ball gag, and a long horse crop that forcefully called my name. Remi came up behind me, dick pressed into my back.

"Pick your poison," he said lowly into my ear. I couldn't decide on one. I wanted to feel them all.

"May I pick more than one?" I asked.

"Yes, you may," he answered. I pointed to the horse crop, paddle, and metal cuffs. Remi cleared everything else off the bed. I didn't move while he did so. Still clad in the robe, I stood there anticipating what would happen next. Jeremiah walked up behind me again. Towering an entire foot above me, I began to feel like I just wanted to melt into his chest. His arms came around me and untied my robe. Listening to it fall to the floor, I looked up into the ceiling, standing there at his mercy. I could feel his breath traveling from my right shoulder up to my hair as he sniffed me like I was his prey. When he came down to my left ear, he let out such an animalistic growl that it made me quiver in both excitement and fear.

"Don't move," he commanded. I stood as still as a blossomed tulip waiting for a breeze to blow by. While stationary, I began to feel the blood rush to every erogenous zone in my body. I wondered where all the equipment came from. Was Remi already a part of this lifestyle and he just didn't say anything, or did he just catch on that quickly? Where was he? What was he doing behind me? The more my mind raced, the higher my temperature rose. I felt him unclasp my bra and slip it off me. He then popped the side of my thong over my skin, snickered and slid them down my legs for me to step out of. Once bare, he stepped away from me. I was frozen with anticipation. While he was seemingly behind me deciding my fate, I tried to relax to not get overly excited. I felt him, once more behind me only this time he came with a hand around my neck. Every bit of fearlessness I held onto slipped out of me right along with the air in my lungs. Remi sounded like such a beast in my ear.

"Mandisa, I have no idea how what you are asking me for works," he paused, breathing in my ear. As he continued, his free hand reached down to rub my clit.

"But if you want me to destroy you, I will break you in the loveliest way possible. I will leave your body soulless from having snatched it through your orgasms. Nobody will hear you screaming."

While he spoke low in my ear and touched me, I moaned ever so softly, awaiting his every word. My clit slid through his

93

index and middle fingers like a credit card having to be swiped several times but slowly. Trying to hold in my excitement I held in my whimpers and let him keep speaking.

"I'll own you, Mandisa. Like my club, like my cars, like this house, like this bed I'm about to impale you in, you'll be my property. Is that really what you want?" he asked. I didn't delay answering.

"Yes. God, yes Jeremiah. Please," I begged. The second I agreed, destruction began. Where I thought he would lick, he bit: the back of my neck, my shoulders and between the blades. I could barely squirm or twist as a witness in my own devouring. An excruciating pain shot through me. As I screamed to the top of my lungs, he continued to apply pressure with his teeth and rub my pussy harder. I was enamored with the feeling of pain I was receiving. In some strange, twisted way it gave me peace in a storm that existed within my body. When he was confident a contusion would show up the next day, he unlocked his jaws from my shoulder and turned me to face him. He cupped my face in his hand, hypnotizing me with his chestnut brown eyes.

"Kneel," he demanded. My entire soul began to sway as my knees buckled from under me and hit the floor as he said. I looked up at this god of a man and followed his gaze as he bent down to meet me face to face. He yanked a handful of my hair, licked the side of my face, and whispered sweet devastation in my ear.

"I'm going to love breaking you," he bellowed. My lungs released an exhale tangled within a soft moan. Remi took my hands and placed them on his abdomen as he stood over me. I lowered my head in obeisance as he took my arms and cuffed them in front of me. The restriction soothed me. The chill of the metal locked around my wrists quickly dissipated by the warmth of my body - A clear contrast from the silk necktie Aziz used. My eyes remained glued shut as I awaited his next command. A leaf hanging on to a limb for dear life at the end of Autumn had more stability than I did. His hand clutched my underarm as he lifted me to my feet. I stood naked, shaking yet unafraid of where I was about to go.

"Look at me," I heard. Opening my eyes, I connected with him and for a moment, only he existed. I wanted to worship him like he was God himself. The darkness of the room married the lust circulating through it. He spoke passionately to me as he circled around me - my juices running down my thighs. There was no other authority but him. With his foot, he spread my legs apart and I stood there as a soldier would at ease. I didn't take my eyes off him for one second.

"Stand straight, hold that pussy open for me and don't move," he said. My soft welcomed my fingers as I immediately split her lips exposing my anticipating clit, throbbing harder than my heartbeat. Shock came over me as he lowered himself as if he was the submissive and extended his warm, wet tongue curling it around my clit repeatedly. My legs tensed up while I looked to the ceiling trying to keep my composure. His tongue was softer than I remembered. I don't know how he expected me to stand there handcuffed, holding my pussy open without collapsing. The more his tongue enveloped my clit, the closer I came to orgasm. I forcibly shook above him. It didn't take long before my body responded accordingly.

"Remi, I'm cumming," I cried. He didn't vocally respond as I orgasmed. He simply looked up at me and kept tasting the honey that dripped from my well. The urge to release what seemed to take me all day to build up swaddled me and I quickly moved my hands to lightly push Jeremiah's head back.

"Baby, wait! I feel like...just wait, please, I'm..." I moaned. In the darkness, I could still make out the grin on his face as he stood up, knowing exactly what I was trying to convey to him.

"I didn't tell you to let go," he growled, pushing me to sit down on the bed, hands still cuffed in front of me. He stood in between my legs and grabbed my neck, bellowing in my ear.

"I said hold your pussy open and don't...move. Let whatever you need to go, go. But keep that pussy open and don't move." he commanded, pushing me all the way down on the bed and positioning my feet on it to support my legs. Tears began welling up as I reached down to reopen the doors he was determined to walk through as he went back to eating. The feeling was almost foreign as it was not what I remembered from our time in college. It was better. Remi had definitely elevated his skills. After the 3rd climax, I couldn't take it any longer, yet I held my pussy open begging him to let me let go.

"Baby please..." I pleaded. "Please, may I let go?" Remi

slowly raised up letting a low growl break free from his core like a lion closing in on its kill. He released the cuffs from around my wrists and let me touch his body. His arms were solid and strong. I gripped them tight as he came up to let me experience what I tasted like. My hands traveled across his back, to the nape of his neck, to holding his face as we passionately kissed each other. While we kissed, the head of his staff kissed my lips down below ever so gently too. My body longed to feel him inside me, yet he raised up and flipped me over on my belly and slapped my ass with his hand firmly before standing up.

"Face down. Ass up. Now," he demanded. I did what I was told with much haste, assuming the position with gratification. Inhaling and exhaling deeply, I awaited what he was about to do. If Remi didn't know what he was doing, I sure couldn't tell within that moment. The way he spoke to me, the way he talked to me, the way he bridged the paddle perfectly with my ass - Jeremiah loved on me like he'd been a Dom for years.

His paddle cracked against my skin again, this time with a harder snap. My spine sprung my body upward and I jumped forward, yelping. Remi's warm hand created a firm grip around the back of my neck as he pushed me back down and held me there. I heard him release a heavy exhale. His free hand softly caressed the point of impact.

"Such a pretty ass..." he grinned. A silence fell into the room as to make space for the loudness that would come immediately after. I could hear the air gathering around the paddle as he took another swing. I clenched the sheets and bit my bottom lip to keep from screaming too loud. Remi halted the sting by rubbing his equally warm hand over the instantly forming welt. The paddle play went on until his sheets were soaked from my orgasms. I was nearly spent as he turned me on my back and slid inside my drenched walls. The scream that tore through my larynx could have shatter glass as my legs hugged him tight as to try to stop him from going deeper. He immediately swatted my attempts to push him back.

"Nah, gimme this pussy. You knew my dick was big before you got here," he asserted. An electrical current rolled through me as I felt him reach the corner of my pussy. I gasped and held my breath to allow the thunder that followed to roll through my body.

96

Pausing briefly, Remi held his position, shook his head, and let it bow into my neck before restarting his stroke. I knew it was good to him by the primal sounds that came from his core. There were growls and grunts that would have intimidated most prey and even some predators. But I embraced it. I welcomed his animalistic behavior. My legs opened wider to fit every inch inside me. I could feel my eyes crossing with every stroke and he clasped my hands into his and put my arms over my head. The stroke was intense.

It was long. It was steady. It was...

Remi-

It was everything I remembered and more. Mandisa felt
amazing. The second I slipped into her warm walls I had to pause,
or I was going to nut right that second. When I gathered myself, I
grabbed her hands and put them above her head to position myself
for greatness. Mandisa was so soft and wet around me, I could feel
her pussy tightening around me every single time she came. Her
moans and screams complimented the passion in which I was fucking her. I was deep inside her with no remorse.

"I love how your legs go in the air. Your pussy feels so
good. It feels like you needed me here. I love how you let me in -
how you let me all the way in there. No pushing me out. You want
all of it. I love it."

"Jeremiah, I'm cummin'!" she screamed. The way she
convulsed beneath me could have cracked the ground had she been
laying on it. My tone stayed consistently low as she came down
from her peak.

"That's a good girl," I approved. I slowed my stroke down
and went deeper as I continued to speak to her.

"You like how I long dick you? How good?" I continue to
whisper.

"SO good," she moaned. Mandisa began panting, trying
to gather her breathing. She began rolling her hips to rub her clit
against my body. I extended her right arm outward and began
tongue kissing her neck, giving her space to bring herself to climax
again. Back-to-back orgasms were like high tides crashing into the
sand, washing away all the disappointment of our past lovers. She
was my savior. I became her god. Her legs lifted higher in the air to
worship me while her nails scratching glory into my skin became
the salvation I needed.

I sat up, reaching for her neck, gripping firmly. Her eyes
were glossed over yet she was completely cognizant of what was
happening. It was as if she had transitioned from helpless prey to
the most powerful being in the room. And she was. Her whines and
cries became 'yes Daddy's and 'fuck me like you love me's. And I
did - both fucked her and loved her. Controlled her and worshipped

98

her. Smutted her out and cherished her.

There was a hint of sinister in the grin she wore on her face. I was throwing wild dick you only find in jungles, and she was taking it like a champ. I briefly pulled out to turn her over and slid right back in those apple pie warm walls of hers. I held her down at the neck and put my whole dick in the corner of her pussy and hit a left. As prissy as she was, she was never a pillow princess. She fucked me just as wild as I fucked her. "Threw it back" was an understatement. I almost didn't recognize her in that moment. She had definitely evolved sexually. This wasn't the quiet Deesie I used to fuck in college. This was Mandisa and the energy seeping from her body demanded that I treat her as such.

She went quiet. Not like she wasn't enjoying it but more so as if she was in a different head space. Her words became slurred and melted together. The gush of wetness all over my dick told me that she experienced another bodily explosion. Though she tried to keep going, her body lost all strength.

"Sssh. It's ok baby. Just lay there and let me fuck you. Let me do all the work,' I encouraged. She slowly surrendered to the smoothness of the silk sheets she came all over and let me have my way with what little life she had left. The way it looked like she was enjoying every bit of it took me to a different level of beast mode. If this is the animal she wanted, she was for sure getting it. The only sound in the room was our bodies crashing into each other. Her legs shook as I touched spots she forgot existed within her. The sensation drew me closer to cum. I whispered to her:

"Where you want this nut?" I thought for sure she was going to say in her walls, and I was fully prepared to give it to her too, but her response shocked the living hell out of me.

"Down...my...throat," she panted. I almost called her a filthy bitch in excitement, but I remained composed, pulled out and turned her back over. I stood as she turned to hang her head over the bed, opening her mouth and sticking out her tongue to receive me. She sucked her juices off and jerked my dick simultaneously. All I could do was hold my head back. Mandisa moaned on my dick like she loved what she was doing. I know she felt me throbbing in her mouth as I was inching closer to my nut. My entire body locked up where I stood as she sucked every bit of soul and life force that co-mingled with the nut I shot to the back of her throat. I could have blown that woman's head off with how hard she made me nut. She moaned louder and sucked harder and then kept sucking even after both sacks were completely emptied into her mouth and my spirit lie naked at her feet. I had to yank myself back and mush her head to get her off me.

"You got it all, nasty!" I exclaimed. I heard her swallow hard and giggle, slowly shifting her body back on the bed. I climbed over her and laid behind her. We stayed in that position for a few seconds until I noticed her breathing pattern change. It went from labored, to steady to tantric. She had zoned out, staring into one of the candles I had lit on the dresser. I'd never seen a woman in such a trance. I didn't know what to do with it at first. She didn't respond to me calling her name nor my hands rubbing her down. She was on a different frequency. This must have been the subspace she was speaking of. I remembered the things she said she needed back on the terrace and gave her all of it. Soft touches, warm embraces, a low whisper if I spoke – She laid still in the protection of my arms.

A little while later, I felt her sit up. Waking me up from a light sleep, I held my head up and asked if she was ok. She didn't respond verbally. She did, however, look in my direction, climbed over me and wrapped her arms around me, burying her face in my back. She let out a deep exhale and drifted back to her space. She didn't move the rest of the night. And there I was: a big, strapping young lad now the little spoon.

Mandisa –

The next morning came in a blur. I don't think I moved all
night. The best part about it was neither did Remi. He was still in
my arms when I woke up. I kissed his back with softness. He took
my hand and pulled my arm further around him.

"Good morning," he yawned. The room was still dark, save
for the little bit of sunlight trying to sneak passed the black out curtains. We laid there in sweet silence for a short while until finally
he rolled over.

"How you feel?" he asked. I smiled and shook my head
in slight disbelief. It was everything I remembered plus tax. Electricity still surged through me in that very moment. He stared into
my eyes with vulnerability. It was almost like he was anticipating
a negative response from me. My eyes became fixated on his in
attempt to figure out where he was mentally and emotionally. I
took his face in my hand and realized what had transpired. While
he performed immaculately, this was new territory for him. He
had never sexed in the capacity of a Dominant. He was unhinged
and out of order the night before. This was the first time he was
enveloped in such control that resulted in a loss of his power and it
rendered him helpless.

"Sir..." I called. I paused in apprehension as the honorific
seemed to slip from my lips as if it were a piece of fruit saturated
in sugar syrup and I tried to grab a handful. I held my breath awaiting his response – never taking my eyes off him.

"Yes, Maze?" he acknowledged.

"Maze?", I smiled, slightly cocking my head back.

"Yea. Maze. I think that's what I want to rename you," he
replied.

"Why Maze?"

"Because I got lost in you. There are so many turns and
directions in which I could go, and I just kept letting my body lead
the way."

"I like that."

"That and you're just amaze-ing," he answered.

"Oh my God, you're so corny!" I laughed, softly pushing

101

him off me. Laughing with me, he pulled me back closer to him and draped my leg over him. A look of seriousness began to trickle down over his face.

"Was it everything you needed, Maze?" he asked. The slight tremble in his voice was confirmation of uncertainty in himself. He was looking for validation and reaffirmation in the space we held for each other. I was sure to give it to him.

"And more, Sir. Truth be told, I thought I was going to come here and put it on you. I swore I was going to buss that ass, Remi. I promise you, I did. And you just...decided otherwise. You've always given the most amazing sex I've ever had and last night was everything I needed," I assured him. It was as if a ton of bricks had been lifted off his chest after hearing me say that. I could see the color come back into his face.

"I'm glad, baby. This is different. Way different. My only goal was to help you get your life, and..."

"And I did," I interrupted.

"Good. I feel better about it," he said. All the air had been cleared. There was no anxiety between the two of us – no awkward, uneasy vibes. It was just us. Us amid a blossoming dynamic. With the clasping of our hands and simultaneous closing of our eyes, we had both silently agreed to travel this unchartered road with each other in discovery of who we really were. The math had always been so easy. We just fit each other like hand in glove. There was no work to be done, no "getting to relearn" each other. Everything felt right so I decided to put the final nail in the coffin with a little humor.

"Your breath stinks," I said softly.

"Well, the last thing I had to eat was your pussy so..." he refuted, rolling over on top of me. I slapped his arm with a laughter that quickly turned into a gasp, followed up with a moan as he slid back inside me. He exhaled as if he had been holding the air in his lungs hostage for 3 days and made love to me until the afternoon crept up on us.

Aziz who?

CHAPTER 8
Calm Within the Storm

It had been 3 months since Remi and I reconnected, and it was all gas and no breaks. Our relationship rapidly blossomed into the most holy of sins. It was beautifully dangerous yet chaotically peaceful. Each day we learned something new and every other night we plunged lower in the depths of this lifestyle and defined, for ourselves, what it should look like.

He smoothly stepped into the role of my Dominant and I, his submissive. For starters, I loved to kneel at his feet. In the mornings, before he would go to work, I would wake up before him, make myself presentable and kneel at his side of the bed until he woke up. He always rolled over with a smile, caressed my face, and said "good morning, Maze" with a kiss to my forehead. He would take my hands and have me stand up with him to give me a hug. Immediately heading to the bathroom to pee and brush his teeth, my job then would always be to lay back down and open my legs so he could have breakfast. It was an absolute must for him.

When he had had his fill, he would choose the panties I was to wear for that day. While we maintained our own residencies, I had my own drawer in his house and bought him one for mine as well. I loved to watch him go into my drawer and sift through the undergarments so meticulously. I'd always wondered why he concentrated so hard on it until one day I noticed that the tie he chose to wear one day just happened to match the color of panty he chose. After three days of coordinating panty and tie choices, I was convinced that was his reasoning behind it. If we were in separate places the night before, I was to pick 3 options, send him pictures and he would decide from there. It would always be followed by a pic of my ass being hugged in them as well as one of him in his suit and (matching) tie in reciprocation.

Throughout our days, we would be in constant communication with each other whether it be through text, Facetime or phone calls and it never got old – we never ran out of things to talk about. He loved when I sent him sexy pics of myself in my office or doing any kind of work. I would always send pictures of my breasts or with my shirt open revealing my bra. Or I would FaceTime him from my office with my breasts exposed and his prompt response would always be "Cookies!", with the biggest grin on his face. He called my breasts "cookies" because I have a little mole under my right areola that resembles a chocolate chip. It always tickled me how he never got tired of seeing them. Sometimes I would be flabbergasted because in my mind, these are the same titties he puts in his mouth damn near every night, yet he consistently looked at them as if it were his first time seeing them. It did so much for my confidence.

When it came to everyday choices, and because making decisions would give me an anxiety with a heaping side of headache as I am an overthinker, he made all my small decisions for me. He did the work of weighing out the pros and cons of a situation marrying it with every possible outcome and would explain it all to me in a way I could easily comprehend. I fully let him lead my life as a Dominant would. I wouldn't question it, I wouldn't whine or complain at his decision – I would simply say "Yes, Sir" and do as he told me. His rule extended from where I would go, who I would go with, what I could and couldn't wear, down to the color of my nails when it was time for a fill in. The only aspect of my life he had no control over was my business. He didn't want it. He left all of that to me unless I asked him for help or advice. The only thing he would reprimand me for was doing too much work. If it started to stress me out, I had to immediately clock out and leave. He knew I struggled with anxiety and wouldn't allow anything to trigger it. He was protective in that way.

Our scenes and sessions progressed naturally. It started with soft play: spanks, hair pulling, a bit of choking and transcended to full blown wrestling matches sometimes. I've always been into masochism. It was something about pain that drove me crazy. I loved belts, paddles, and horse crops. It drove me insane when he would pinch my nipples. In his most savage moments, he would leave teeth marks and contusions in places I couldn't explain to my father. I can only compare him to a werewolf or some other beastly mythical being that can't help but to snatch the life from a person.

Sometimes he would get so into his zone that he would slap me across my face and spit in my mouth. It was never a hock spit where he would pull it from deep within him and spew it at my face like you see in hardcore pornography. It was a sensual, sexy slow drip into my mouth. Most times, I would be the one calling for it. I would be under him, looking him square in the eye, open my mouth and stick my tongue out. He knew exactly what to do from there. I would fall in love all over again, every single time. Everything about it was so harmonious. Just like it was in my nature to submit, it was in his to control and he understood the assignment fully.

I didn't have to teach him that to dominate, one must first submit. Remi did nothing to me that I didn't allow him to. He never crossed my boundaries, always performed aftercare if I fell into subspace and learned my body so well, he knew where my threshold for pain ended. He was my servant before I was his submissive. He lived to please me. I thought the pedestal Aziz put me on was high. Man, Remi had me looking down at it. He and I were two gods who hated being on earth but made the best use of our time on it by worshipping and loving on each other.

If I had to classify him in the ranks of Dominants, I would consider him a Soft Dominant. One who doesn't rule with an iron fist because he doesn't have to. When he had to put his foot down, he put it down in a loving way as to not crush my spirit. He never called me names outside of sex, where I loved to be called shit like a "filthy bitch" or "sexy smut". If I made him angry, he would take a minute to decompress and assess what was going on. Even when the brat in me reared her ugly head, I knew not to push him. I called him the "King of Pull Up" because any and every time I tried popping off, he would pop up to wherever I was and put me back in my place like it was nothing. I learned early on when he had to beat his chest at me like he was King Kong one time when I called myself pushing his buttons. I got in my feelings and told him I was leaving the relationship. I had no real reason other than I was in my feelings. He pulled right up to my condo, put his dick to my chest from my honeypot, held it there and in the calmest tone said, "stop playin' wit' me". I hadn't played with him since. I quickly realized that those were not the problems I wanted with him.

Classifying me as a submissive was hard because I was a mix of natural submissive, a pet and even a brat. My submission was out of this world. I was a class 5, Omega level submissive and I knew the power it wielded. Because I'd never felt like any of the classifications truly fit me and because I thrived off breaking rules, I set out to redefine what it was-or at least create my own lane within it. My only priority in life was him. I was compelled to serve him in everything I did. He was a god among men, and

106

I couldn't help but to bow at his feet. I can't stress enough how kneeling was my favorite thing to do. It was in kneeling that I became closest to him. I was connected to the divine when I knelt. I was my softest, most vulnerable self at his feet. There wasn't a care in the world that I had. Everything around me just stopped and it was only he and I in the entire world. Whenever he walked through the door, I jumped out of my skin so happy to see him. I'd be like a little puppy dog waiting for her master to come home. Whenever his name and number popped up on my screen, I smiled from ear to ear. It didn't matter if he had to call me back a few seconds later. I grinned like I hadn't spoken to him all day. However, I also got into moments where I just wanted to give him lip and backtalk because I wanted a specific reaction from him. He would give me a command and instead of simply doing so, I would snap back with "make me". The look on his face after would always turn me on because I knew he would get up and do just that. Everything just worked so seamlessly with us.

The only problem was I wasn't collared yet. In this community, a collar is a sign of ownership and being owned. It shows the world that you belong to someone. It can somewhat be compared to a wedding ring but for people in a Dom/sub relationship. It forms a bond not easily broken. I wanted, so desperately, to be collared by Remi. I ached for everybody to know who I belonged to. The only ones that knew we were a thing were Trinnie, Mozelle and his best friend, Ezra. The girls reveled in the idea of me getting my life in this newfound glory of mine. Seeing the marks and contusions he left on me at times gave them excitement and I would showcase them like trophies. But they were the only two that knew about us other than his colleague. I was proud of my submission. I knew I was a type of woman that most men would love to have. But why wouldn't he collar me? While I chalked it up to him being new to this lifestyle and just not knowing the significance of being collared, most of me wished he understood.

I did know that being collared is not something that should be rushed. Because of the symbolism behind it, two people entering a dynamic such as we had shouldn't do so lightly. But we had years of history. The commitment was already there. There wasn't any more vetting that could possibly be done between us. I was ready to be locked down. But I had to follow his lead, so I chose to remain quiet about it. I knew that when the time really was right, he'd collar me.

Overall though, our relationship was solid. We existed within the chaos surrounding us. There was nothing that could shake us. The world could have been burning around us, but we stood together in blissful peace. Our only focus was each other. We were the calm within the storm.

Remi

      That woman changed my entire world in a course of three
fuckin' months. Mandisa had me doing things and being somebody
you could only imagine in your wildest dreams. She worshipped
me like I created Heaven and Earth and if you asked her, I did. I
created a space for her to be free. She could let her freak flag fly
with me. There was nothing she could ask me for that I deemed too
disgusting. I was a little thrown off the first time she wanted me
to spit in her mouth, though. She didn't outrightly say "spit in my
mouth". She simply looked me in my eyes, stuck her tongue out
and something in me just knew that's what she wanted. If I recall
correctly, I nut in her walls four seconds after it drizzled down her
throat because, oddly enough, it turned me on.
      She loved to be at my feet, too. It gave her much peace and
privilege to be my possession. When we'd be watching television,
she wouldn't sit next to me. She would sit beneath me naked or
with panties on and crouch downward with her exquisite ass in the
air in front of me, resting her head on her folded arms – and would
be utterly content and quiet watching whatever I was watching.
      Hearing "yes, Sir" when I gave her something to do
sparked a lust within me I almost couldn't control. And when I was
deep in her guts, caving her walls in, it became "yes, Master", even
though we didn't consider her a slave. She knew how to snatch a
soul. Her submission to me gave me strength. I didn't know what
drove her to serve me the way she did because all I did for her
was give her room to grow. I only did what she asked of me. She
needed someone to control her - I told her what to do. She required
management - I managed all aspects of her except her work, and
even then, if I saw it was overwhelming for her, I shut it down and
told her to come home. She needed someone to fuck her regally – I
made her a goddess. There was nothing on the planet that I didn't
or couldn't give Mandisa. She was the only woman who gave it
up the way I needed and could take it the way I tossed it. She was
wild and it worked perfectly because I was just as wild.
      She was big on the Love Languages – very adamant about
me learning what they were, what hers was and what mine was

and made a conscious effort to speak mine every single day. Mine turned out to be physical touch and acts of service. I loved to put my hands on her and feel hers on mine. She would randomly send me pictures of her body every day and I would never get bored. I'd be at the club punching numbers, getting aggravated about spending too much on certain things and in comes a photo of her cookies, right on time. She had a cute little mole that reminded me of a chocolate chip, and I loved putting them in my mouth so "cookies" was the only thing that fit in naming her tits. Sometimes she would video call me completely naked while I was in a meeting, catching me completely off guard but I loved it. I never missed her call. It didn't matter where I was or what I was doing. If she called my phone, I'd answer.

She had no type of filter or couth and didn't care who heard what she would say or saw her body and I didn't either. I'd often be in my office or in one of the sections of my club before opening going over management of the night when she would video call me. My best friend and managing partner, Ezra would be sitting right next to me and could see everything going on. When she would spot him, she'd tell me he was looking and asked me to move my head so he could better see and would start playing with her pussy telling me how she can't wait for me to get home so I could split her open. When I would look back, I'd see him just staring with his jaw to the floor. I couldn't help but to chuckle and shake my head, going back to my work.

"Maze, he needs to focus on the numbers so I can get you those new shoes you wanted, baby. Put your pussy up until I get home," I would say. She would always suck her teeth, roll her eyes, huff and puff and fuss about how I would never let her have any fun. Ezra could never believe it. It never bothered me that he knew what her body looked like or that she liked teasing him. Her radical friends had seen my dick swinging in the camera as well and we never made it weird. It didn't have to be. We were both adults in a healthy relationship. We gave no room to doubt or jealousy.

Maze was fun to be with. She unlocked a part of me I never knew existed. She always made me look and feel like a god walking the earth. In turn, I brought her to her highest potential. Before me, she was always so tough and crass with people. When I got a hold of her, her energy shifted in a way that allowed her to be softer and not so guarded and I did everything for her that created a space for that brand of energy to thrive. She told me about her ex and how he spoiled her, but it was nothing compared to the life I provided for her.

Her pussy was always my first meal of the day. Whereas most men would be selfish in that arena, Maze deserved her pussy sucked every single morning. I would start her days off with orgasms. She knew the drill. I would wake up to her at my bedside ready to serve me. One would think they'd want someone like that to wait on them hand and foot as a slave would, but Maze was nowhere comparable to my slave. That woman was the air I breathed. Her serving me in the mornings consisted of her thick ass thighs being open while she exposed her clit for my tongue to say good morning to. I never needed to bust a nut, though most times she would crave me cumming in her mouth after making her cream so hard in mine. Sometimes I would give it to her, others I would leave her hungry for me until I got back home but she never started her days unsatisfied.

Her effort and her want to please me is what did it for me. It superseded all the women before and in between her. No one did it the way she did it. She gave me peace – often the remedy for everyday bullshit. I looked to her to relieve my stress just by her excitement to see me when I walked through the door. My days were always long and most times exhausting, and Maze relieved it all. I named her "Maze" because that's exactly what she was: a maze. So many sides, twists and turns to her. She goes so deep, it's easy to get lost in her beautiful labyrinth. She was never loud – never nagged. She would always make my house feel like home.

The only downside I saw to our relationship was my inexperience in being a Dominant. I got the basic concept of it but there was so much more that I knew Maze wanted and needed from me. I had no problem with providing it for her, but I often wondered was what I was giving her enough. Yes, she was satisfied sexually but was she content mentally, emotionally, and spiritually was my question. I cared about all those aspects of her. There was no question as to whether I cherished her or not. We were both wet behind the ears with the whole idea of kink but if Maze wanted it, Maze got it.

I understood that her submission to me was my responsibility. I was responsible for her well-being. I was always careful in the words I spoke to her as her Love Language was always Words of Affirmation. Words could either make or break her and her words could either build up or tear down so when it came to having to discipline the brat in her, I did it lovingly. I always corrected her negative behavior with a stern yet caring tone.

There was one time, though, where I had to use aggression when reigning her back in. One time she called me, upset because she made up in her mind that I was still fucking one of my bottle girls because she saw the way the chick looked at her every time she came to the club and told me she was leaving me. At the time, I was out and about getting supplies for work and decided to take a little detour by her place to see if she'd say she was leaving to my face. The concierge knew who I was, so he didn't waste time in making me sign in and call upstairs. I got to her door and knocked. While I could have used the key she'd given me, I needed her to be a little shook when she came to the door. When she opened it, her eyes widened and gave me the satisfaction I was looking for. I walked in, taking my suit jacket off.

"Now, what were you saying?" I asked, unfastening my cufflinks. I didn't take my eyes off her for one second. Her faltering was like watching the entire world collapse in on itself.

"I...I..." she stuttered, stumbling back into the door. After I loosened my tie and took it off, I stretched my neck and grabbed her by hers.

"I need to know what you were saying, Maze," I growled, squeezing harder. I kissed her lips softly, backing her into the door further. Her muffled pleas made my dick hard. The more she stammered, the more I was going to enjoy checking her. Truth be told, I was annoyed and upset that she would even think of leaving me and my feelings were slightly hurt by it, but I kept kissing her passionately. She was wearing one of my tee shirts, so I pulled her leg up with one hand and pulled my dick out with the other. Her breathing pattern became labored. She knew what was coming for her.

"Daddy...Daddy wait. Master...Sir...", she begged. Maze called out every honorific she could to avoid punishment for what she said. I bathed in her petitions like it was early morning baptism. I pulled the lace panties I chose for her to the side and slid every inch of my dick to the back of her warm, tight pussy.

"What were you saying, Maze?" I demanded. I stroked her slowly, up against the door. She couldn't do anything but moan, but I needed answers. With my dick still balls deep inside her, I guided her to the floor. I held her legs back, putting my weight on her so she couldn't run and drilled that good pussy until kingdom cum. When I felt like I was getting through to her, I pressed further inside her until there was no more pussy to fuck and held it there. She writhed in agonizing pleasure. I squeezed her cheeks together with one hand and let the dominance show in my face before I uncompromisingly hissed in her ear.

"Stop...playin' wit' me, Mandisa," I grunted through my teeth. "You love me. I love you. I'm not goin' nowhere. You not goin' nowhere. I'm not fuckin' that girl and I'm 'bout to nut all in this pretty pussy," and exploded inside her without a care. I continued to hold it there while every drop of my soul dripped into her.

"Are we clear?" I asked. She faintly nodded as I let her face go.

"Good girl. I'll be back later," I asserted as I got up, fixed myself and went back to my errands. I got a text message from her a few minutes later saying "I'm sorry I accused you. It won't happen again". I thought about whether or not I had done the right thing during my entire shift. I didn't want to hurt her, but I needed the message to be clear: that leaving shit was a no-go for me. You leave, you gotta stay gone. I had real issues with people I loved in my life that left me and I wasn't about to just let her walk away. But was I too aggressive? The thought plagued me until I left the club. That night when I got back to her place, I apologized for being so forceful with her and made it up to her by kneeling at her feet. To be the one who dominated this goddess, I had to first put myself in her position. I had to willfully submit to her so I could understand where she was mentally, spiritually, and emotionally. It was in that moment that I realized everything that Mandisa was sacrificing but I also recognized what she was gaining in her surrender. Although I was the one in control, she was the one with all the power. Comprehending the exchange blew my mind.

I thought about it constantly – thought about her constantly. She became an obsession. The more she served me, the higher I wanted to build her plinth. Her love was incomparable. I've never had anything like it. I knew she was different back in college, but her caliber of distinction was unmatched. I simply had to give this woman every bit of me I could. There were no bounds with her - no limit in how far I was willing to go to please her.

I sat at my desk thinking about how I could show her I was serious about embracing this lifestyle with her. Although I was still wet behind the ears, she had patience with me. Again, we were both learning the ropes and navigating these uncharted waters together. She confessed to me that her ex was the one that piqued her interest in BDSM, but she didn't really feel as though she could fully let her freak flag fly with him. Leading into this moment, I would listen to her tell me how she felt this way even in college. She didn't know what the feeling was and often felt like something was wrong with her. She really didn't get to experience the full lifestyle due to the abrupt ending of their relationship. That man was a fool but I'm glad he fucked up. Maze was mine for the taking. But how was I going to take her to her next level?

My thoughts were interrupted by Ezra barging into my office unannounced with a file in his hand, mentioning the quarterly budget. We were a bit under, which explained his enthusiastic pace.

"Yo, my guy," he grinned. "Have you gone over the numbers yet?"

"Nah, not yet. Talk to me."

"We're coming in at just five grand under. Getting that new promoter was a good look. He keeps this place packed," he rejoiced. I took the file from him to review.

"Yea, I agree. We have to figure out what to do about Mondays though. I want to be open seven days a week."

"Seven days?! Breh, that's madness. I won't be volunteering for that."

"You're probably right. Mandisa would kill me."

"Breh, since when do you worry about what a chick would say?"

"Since her," I replied. Ezra looked intrigued.

"Breh, where do you find these broads?!", he asked emphatically.

"Watch ya mouth. She aint no broad," I said. The hood jumped out of me in wanting to protect who Mandisa was. I watched as light left his eyes, becoming filled with more questions.

114

"Yea fine, whatever. But yo…you stay with a chick flashin' you her titties at random. Bro, you da Pussy Whisperer," he exclaimed. All I could do was laugh and even blush a little because he wasn't telling lies. I did have the innate ability to finesse a woman's panties off at will. It wasn't something I was overly proud of, but it was what it was.

"Nah man, Maze is different," I said. "That girl got some witch pussy, I swear." We both laughed.

"Yea, I bet! The way you be around here zoned out!" chuckled Ezra.

"I can't help it. She does sumn' to me. I can't get her out of my mind," I confessed.

"Her pussy that good, bro?"

"Yea it is but it's way more than that. She just got this magic about her. She makes me want to give her everything. She knows how to put it on. I just think about her, and my dick goes stiff," I explained. A look of disgust instantly draped Ezra's face.

"Aight, aight yo damn. I aint wanna hear about ya dick. Stop tossin' that shit everywhere. She into that freaky shit though, aint she?" he inquired.

"Yea. It's called BDSM."

"Billy D, what now?" he asked confusingly. I laughed in response.

"B…D…S…M. Stands for Bondage, Dominance, and Sadomasochism, among other things," I expounded. Ezra looked so perplexed.

"…the hell you mean 'among other things?! What other things?" he queried. I embraced the teachable moment with my chest poked out.

"Well in our case, the D and S stands for dominance and submission. I'm…"

"Yo, you be puttin' her in full Nelson's, breh?!" he interrupted.

"No dummy. I'm her Dominant and she's my submissive. That's all it means."

"Nah that aint all that means. Spill it," he probed. I spent the next ten minutes divulging some of the details of the nature of our relationship, careful not to expose too much. Though enthralled, it was not Ezra's cup of brandy, and it was clear. I did,

115

however, confide in him that I was a little stumped in how I wanted to take it further with Maze.

"Breh, how much further can you go? That's already extreme," he said.

"It's unfathomable, my friend. And we're just at the tip of the iceberg, dude. You'd be surprised at what people like. I did my homework on this and dude I'm tellin' you – what we've dived into is shallow waters. But she's not scared to tread deeper and I'm not afraid to lead her there. I just don't know how I want to do it."

"Well, get ya feet wet over there. I'll watch from afar if ya'll need me to, but it has to be…afar. That shit is crazy," he scoffed. Ezra just didn't get it and that was ok. I understood it wasn't for everybody. As our conversation ended, he picked up his folder and headed downstairs to receive the shipment of liquor he'd ordered for the house. I remained in my chair, bobbing back and forth in contemplation. Hands clasped together and index fingers poking my chin, I thought long and hard on what it would take to get to the next level.

Maze had always been a masochist. Coupled with this newfound urge to be watched, ideas started circulating in my head. "I'll watch from afar" played in my mind repeatedly. I wondered would Ezra be game to watch Maze get her ass handed to her that night. It was a Friday, so she didn't have to work the next morning. I grabbed my phone to text her.

"Be in my bed by time I get home," I typed. Glowering at my phone, I could hear my staff starting to trickle in. The bottle girls giggled, trapsing to their dressing room. My bartenders yelled to each other from across the hall and my security bellowed in laughter over not having a repeat of the night before. My evening was about to start. As I raised from my seat, my phone alerted me to a message. "Yes, Sir," was all I needed to read. Now, to get Ezra on board.

The night went on smoothly. Rasa was packed from wall to wall, the bottle girls were switching back and forth hurriedly and everyone was just having a good time. Ezra and I sat in my office just watching everything unfold with scotch in our glasses. I figured this would be the best time to offer the proposition.

"What would you say if I asked you to watch me and Maze tonight?". The room suddenly became small. The only thing visible

116

to my eyes was the vibration of the glass against the muffled bass my DJ was knocking. I could hear the shock in Ezra's voice.

"Breh, what?" he asked. I turned my head to him and repeated myself.

"What would you say if I asked you to watch me and Maze tonight?"

"Are you serious? I literally just told yo ass to stay o... ver...there with that shit. Now you want me to watch? Deadass?"

"Deadass. I'll give you a minute to think about it," I replied, turning my head back to the crowd outside my window. He paused, briefly mulling over the idea. I saw him take a short sip of his drink, then throw the whole glass back.

"Fuck it, I'm down," he said. I continued to show no emotion as I peered through the window, drink glass rubbing back and forth across my bottom lip. I was in deep thought. Images of what I was going to do to Maze when I got home flashed across my mind.

"Whatever you see tonight...don't flinch," I warned Ezra. Turning my head back to him, I could see a hint of dread in his face. We were about to give him a show he'd never forget. I raised my glass to him, finished my drink and headed downstairs to join the crowd leaving him to his thoughts.

Mandisa

The sun was just beginning to come up as I stood at the mirror staring at all the welts Remi left on my body with his belt. They were so beautiful. My raised skin looked like vibrant swipes of red paint across it. My body became a masterpiece. My back, ass and thighs were covered in ridges. I was standing there zoned out in subspace draped in Remi's sheets. Ezra had just left minutes prior and I was still shaking from all the impact my body received but I had to see it for myself. The second Remi came back upstairs from seeing his friend out, I collapsed in his arms. He carried me to the bed and began icing me down.

"You did so well, baby," he encouraged. As I was coming down from my high, the sensation began to come back to my body, and I began to feel the sting from the aftermath of Remi's leather belt. The scene was intense yet so fulfilling.

I received a text from him earlier, the evening before, telling me to be in his bed by time he got home from the club. I was on the couch with Trinnie when it came through. As I read it, I jumped up and told her I had to go. Frantically grabbing the necessities, Trinnie watched me run around like a chicken with its head cut off and one foot without offering her help. I heard my front door open and close with Mo walking through it, perplexed as to why I was in a panic.

"Remi texted her," revealed Trinnie.

"Ah, I see," Mo responded as she plopped down on my couch. They both sat there talking amongst themselves as I anxiously finished gathering my things.

"I aint never seen this bitch that beat over dick," said Trinnie.

"Mmm mm! Neither have I. She beat beat." I had to interrupt them both in desperation. Although I had time, Remi was known to pull up at any given time and I didn't want to chance not being there when he said.

"Will you bitches stop cackling and help me get out the door?!" I snapped. Mo enjoyed watching me sweat. The smirk on her face was remarkable. As they both got up, Trinnie grabbed me by the shoulders.

"Relax. That penis aint goin nowhere," she assured. While she was trying to be helpful, she didn't understand the severity of it all. I had to be on time. I needed to be on time. Mo understood what it was though. We've had extensive conversations about it. She knew exactly where my mind and heart were so while she chuckled at my pain, she also began to help me get ready. When I was all set and headed to the door, I blew the girls kisses and left them on my couch.

The drive over was short and sweet. I had plenty of time to jump in the tub and relax because Rasa didn't close until 2 in the morning. Running the faucet, I let my sweat suit fall to the floor. The towels were freshly laundered, and the smell was so crisp as I sniffed one before wrapping my head in it. My silk robe he gave me the first night we reconnected, made its home on the back of the bathroom door so I clad myself in it briefly to allow the water to fill the tub. It was boiling hot, as steam wafted off the surface. The ivory-colored tile was a comforting contrast to the black and gold marble floor. Testing the water with my fingertips, I disrobed and stepped into the liquid fire. I hung my arms over the sides of the tub and inhaled the eucalyptus fumes from the bubbles. My mind and body began preparing themselves for whatever Remi had in store. After bathing, I dried off, put my smell goods on and slipped into a black cami for Remi to take off when he got home. There was nothing left to do but wait. I had a couple of books to read to help the time pass and as it pressed on, unable to truly focus on the trashy paperback, I peacefully drifted to sleep in his bed to thoughts of him circulating through my head.

In what felt like days later, I hear the door crack open. I was still half asleep, so I just laid there waiting for him to climb into bed next to me. Hearing him walking around, I also heard what I perceived to be furniture moving around but I paid no attention to it. After a short time, his footsteps ceased and there was nothing but silence. I could feel his eyes undressing me. The seconds felt like minutes that felt like hours before the warmness of his comforter began dragging down my body until they plopped to the floor. I curled up slightly to escape the chill that came over my body. There was a few more seconds of silence until Remi's hand wrapped around my ankle, yanking me to the edge of his bed.

It startled me slightly, but his voice is what sent me in a frenzy.

"Get up," he commanded. I placed my feet to the floor to get a proper footing yet stumbled slightly in sleepiness. Remi's arms felt like one of my grandmother's hand-knitted sweaters hugging me. I stood there allowing myself to get lost in his embrace. My back was buried in his chest while his hands wandered all over me. I rested my head back on his shoulder and let him touch me. His fingertips were like velvet across my skin. He smelled like power and respect had twins together. I was enthralled by how solid he felt – like a brick wall with a 9 ½ inch dick that curved to the left. Remi had me wide open. I imagined a secluded space, void of any interruption from the outside world. It was just he and I, alone – free to get as wild as…as…wait…who the fuck is that?!

I just so happened to raise my head and open my eyes to see a dark figure sitting in Remi's chair at the end of the room, but it wasn't Remi. Apprehension filled my body as I turned my head with fear in my eyes.

"Daddy…who…"

"Sssssh. Relax baby. That's Ezra. He's just here to watch," whispered Remi. What was he doing here? Was he just going to watch, or did he anticipate some action as well? Though I wasn't opposed to him being there, his presence caught me off guard. Pressure began to build up in my head and I became slightly dizzy. Everything began to move so fast. This was a fantasy of mine that Remi was bringing into fruition. My fearful panting slowly calmed into measured, melodic breathing. I didn't take my eyes off Ezra as Remi's right hand roamed to my honey well while his left clenched my throat. I could tell Ezra was enjoying the view.

I was unsure if it was because his boy was there or I was just super horny, but Remi's fingers rubbing my pussy felt buttery soft that night. I moaned in sweet satisfaction; eyes still glued to Ezra. I wanted more. I wanted him to get a closer look at what was happening to me. Being in the corner while all of that glorious unraveling was happening in front of him wasn't fair.

"Sir, may I have a word with Ezra?" I asked. Remi's lips touched my neck softly, leaving kisses in their trail.

"Absolutely Maze, have all the words you need," he said. His attention then shifted to his boy.

"Ezra, Maze would like to talk to you," he encouraged.

Ezra was taken aback as he jumped up and looked around as if there was another Ezra in the room that Remi could have been talking to. While Remi kept pleasing my awakening pink, I insisted that Ezra come to me so that I could talk to him.

"I don't bite. Come here Ezra. Please," I whimpered. He came forward and stood before me. I looked up at him as he was taller than me and licked my lips coating them with lust. Remi gripped my neck tighter and rubbed me sweetness more vigorously. My body started to charge up. Power began to surge through me as I watched Ezra crumble. I knew he'd never been witness to anything of the sorts and I was a curious vixen looking to have fun because neither had I. But even in my inexperience, I felt mighty. I was the most powerful being in the room in that moment and I wallowed in all my own glory.

"What you see here tonight, stays here. Whatever my Ruler does to me in this room – know that I constantly ache for it." Moans hopscotched in between my words as I continued.

"Know that...mmm...I asked for this. I...ooo...I...I'm..." I stuttered as I began to feel a climax emerge. Remi must have felt it too and discontinued rubbing on me.

"No. Hold it," he ordered. An extreme concentration of energy began rushing to my clit as Remi edged me devilishly.

"How involved would you like Ezra to be tonight?" he asked. I put my eyes back on Ezra, while catching my breath, as I saw him give Remi a surprising look.

"What's acceptable to you, Daddy?" I answered. Remi continued to kiss on me; his left hand freeing my throat to join his right in coasting all over me.

"Tell me what you want," he requested. Because Ezra was not looking me in the eyes, I grabbed his face by the cheeks and turned his head to me so I could witness his upending. Remi relished in my splendor. He became in love with the way I switched gears on his friend. This was the first time he'd given me a toy to play with and I wanted to enjoy the fun.

"Can he touch me if I want?" I inquired. Remi kept kissing me slowly in between answering me.

"I'll allow it."

"Can he kiss me?" I felt the straps from my cami fall off my shoulders as Remi pulled it down, exposing my breasts.

"I'll allow it."

"Can he taste me?" My eyes stabbed a gaping hole into Ezra's soul, and I felt my supremacy heighten as he grew weaker before me. Remi hesitated in answering due to him being entertained by my spine curling at his kiss. He softly chuckled and bit down on my shoulder blade causing me to scream.

"I'll allow it," he rejoined. Ezra was mesmerized. Through panting, I asked one final question with his whole face in my hand: staring him into final surrender to me.

"Can he fuck me, Daddy?" My voice was boisterous and clear. The pain from him biting me triggered a rapid chemical response that sent my body on a frenzy. Ezra was under my spell. I could sense his soul spilling out through his eyes and into my raging pussy. Remi forcefully yanked my head back to rest on his shoulder as he pulled his dick out his slacks and passionately slid it inside me, holding it where it stopped. I felt his face lean on mine.

"Mmm...I'll allow it, Maze," he grunted. While I gasped at the chilling pain that skyrocketed up my body, I was careful not to scream as to not intimidate Ezra any further. I let his face go, as Remi pulled himself out of me, stood back and watched, briefly. Pulling Ezra to my eye level by his necktie, I licked from his chin to his lips, sticking my tongue in his mouth. His was almost as soft as Remi's. I bit his bottom lip and fiendishly giggled, stepping back to let Remi undress me completely. I stood there naked before two of the most gorgeous Black men I have ever seen in my life. I felt my juices dripping down my thighs.

Remi began unbuttoning his sleeves. Ezra followed suit and loosened his tie. I was impressed with his composure. I could tell he was nervous, but he hid it well. Remi continued to undress, watching me pull Ezra's undershirt from over his head and gently pushing him to the bed.

"Lay down, Maze," Remi said. I did as I was told and felt Ezra's warm chest against my back. His heart beat forcefully under his ribcage. He was a little tense and it amused me. I told him gently to relax. Although he was shirtless, he still had his pants on, but I rubbed his hard staff with my soft ass anyway. I watched my Ruler fully undress and stand at the foot of the bed like the god he was.

"Hold her legs back," he said. I felt Ezra, rough hand run

down my thighs and spread them apart gripping them as he did so. Remi then fixed his eyes on me.

"Keep em open," he asserted.

"Yes, Sir," I obliged. Reaching down, I split my pussy lips open, the way he liked it, and let my clit welcome his tongue home. While he tasted me, the sensation of Ezra's kiss to my neck gently crept its way into the picture. I slowly closed my eyes and let the feeling wash over me. I couldn't explain what was happening, but I knew I didn't want it to stop. I moved my head back and beckoned Ezra to kiss me. Our lips touching sent off fireworks in my brain. As we both fell into the pool of bliss we were creating, Remi began sucking on my clit causing Ezra and I's embrace to break briefly. I jumped and my legs sprung closed. Remi grinned almost maliciously, lifting himself off the bed to instruct Ezra.

"Nah Ezra, you gotta hold them thighs tight. They're thick and strong. Don't let em get away from you. She got a habit of squirming when it gets too good to her," he boasted. Ezra nodded his head in compliance and yanked my legs back with a firmer grip.

"Heard you," he said resuming his kisses on me. Remi went back to putting my entire cunt on his nose. I moaned in agreement to his will. I leaned back again, this time sticking my tongue out for Ezra to suck on. We kissed zealously as I let stifled moans escape from me. The urge to cum started to build up again. My hips started to sway in attempt to wiggle themselves out of this feeling, but Ezra's grip was solid. I couldn't move. I broke our kiss once more to plead with Remi.

"Daddy, I'ma mess these sheets up again. Please…" Remi paid no attention to me as to say, 'resistance is futile', applying more suction with his lips. The more I tried to move, the stronger Ezra's hold on me became.

"Ssssh. Let it happen," he murmured. "Be a good girl and cum for him, yea?" The more he spoke, and the faster Remi's tongue spun, the more intense the build up became. I couldn't hold it any longer. I released such a volatile orgasm it shook me to the core. Remi lifted again, this time with my essence dripping from his chin and a huge grin on his face.

"Atta girl," he said. He grabbed my ankle, yanking me to the edge once more.

"Gimme ya belt, Ezra," he roared. Ezra, without hesitation, jumped up and pulled his belt from the loops and handed it to Remi, laying back down. Tossing me on my stomach like a haystack in an open field, he tied the belt around my neck and snatched me up. Wrapping it around his hand once and pulling, he entered my cave of wonders and rubbed the magic lamp. He fucked my pussy so good. Every time I tried to hang my head, he jerked it back up by the belt.

"Nah, you wanted somebody to watch you get fucked gloriously so let him watch. Look at him while I'm fucking you. Don't take your eyes off him. Tell him how good it feels. He wanna know how good it feels. Tell him," he groaned. I couldn't utter a word; just moans, winces, and whimpers as I was getting my back blown out. Ezra looked so captivated. My wails charmed his snake as I could see his print through his pants. I could feel another orgasm blooming. My whining turned into full on sobs and it grew. Somehow Ezra knew I was about to cum because he jumped to my aide and held my face.

"Uh uh. Look at me. Focus Maze. It's just an orgasm. We're right here. Remi's here. I'm here. Focus. Cum. Tell me how good it feels. I wanna know," he directed. The asphyxiation from the leather around my neck became solace. My eyes became heavy as the lack of oxygen to my brain took over. Remi caught sight of it and loosened his grip so that I could breathe again, never once slowing his stroke. He was so skilled at knowing my limits. Ezra saw me slipping away and coached me back to life.

"Stay with me Maze. I know it's intense, I know," he comforted.

"Yea, that's it. Get her to cum for me. Talk her through her nut while I give her all this dick I been holdin' onto for her," praised Remi. I loved the way he talked to me while he fucked me. It was aggressive like he wanted to smut me out but love me at the same time.

After another orgasm, Remi release the belt, leaned down and kissed me fervently before plopping down on the bed to catch his breath. Ezra and I caught each other's gaze once more.

"Ayo, Remi. I wanna see what she tastes like, if she'll let me," he said, keeping his eyes on me. I smiled and got permission from Remi to put it in his face. I fully and completely consented once I had it and laid down. Though not as soft as Remi's, Ezra's tongue felt like a snake with a pillow of clouds wrapping it. I squirmed with excitement. While he ate, my head cocked itself back and my mouth opened, compelling Remi to put his rod in it. I sucked a sweet melody of moans and groans from him. There the 3 of us were: in tantric rhythm with each other.

The vibe slowed down, but the passion remained high. Ezra used his mouth to sooth my pussy from the beating she received moments prior, and I sucked on Remi like I was a maniac until he gushed in my mouth and all over my face. His dick stayed hard even after he climaxed. Getting up off the bed, he stood at its side and watched Ezra continue to eat.

"She tastes good, don't she?"

"Hell yea," answered Ezra. I sat up and supported myself with my elbows, rubbing my nipples. I looked up to see Remi enjoying watching me get served.

After I came in Ezra's mouth, I wanted to see what he felt like inside me. I requested that he undress, sit on the edge of the bed, and let me straddle him once he did. His head falling backwards told me my walls did what they were made to do. He felt amazing inside me. His hands gripped my ass tight as I rocked back and forth on it. The kisses he eloquently left on my collarbone were soft. From what I could tell, his eyes were shut tight, and he was in the zone just enjoying the moment.

My back was met with Remi's hard dick as he reached down to rub my breasts. He then began rubbing all the parts that weren't being rubbed by Ezra's hand. Four hands parading all over my body while I had a hefty sized dick inside me blew my mind. I was in Heaven – completely in a different mental space. And just when I thought it couldn't get any better, Remi held one of my arms out, Ezra, taking his que from him, held the other and in synchronization, bit my forearms like I was the fruit of life. It was a wonder none of the neighbors heard the scream that flung itself out of my mouth.

Remi pulled my torso back, supporting me while he let Ezra long dick me. I wanted to cum so bad and I almost did until Ezra stood up, breaking my concentration. We were a human "H" as Ezra slid back and forth inside me while Remi's dick was tickling my esophagus. I could hear both men moaning in gratification. This was the wildest thing I'd ever been involved in. I had no clue how what we were doing was even aerodynamically possible, but it felt like Remi had already drawn up blueprints for it. I didn't anticipate my body being destroyed so good. Before we all lost balance from the force of gravity between us, Remi lifted me up, having me wrap my arms around Ezra's neck.

"You got her? I wanna try something different," he said.

"Yea, I got her," answered Ezra, standing there bouncing me on his dick while Remi went to the dresser. Ezra's cock hit my spot with a force I can't describe. I told them both I was about to cum again. Remi, from across the room, evenly fumbling through the drawer, cheered me on while Ezra maintained a steady stroke so I could release. When I did, he kissed me and stood tall, catching some air with me still latched on.

"Ayo, what you lookin' for over there?" he asked Remi. Rummaging some more, he found it: the lube. We never really needed it, so my mind began to wonder what he thought he was about to do with that. When he rejoined the party, the devious grin on his face told me he was up to no good.

"Aight Maze. I'ma need you to relax and breathe, ok baby?" he said as I felt the cold lube and his warm finger massage my asshole. Ezra saw the look of worry in my face. It wasn't the first time we've done anal, but it would be my first double penetration, so I became slightly anxious. As afraid as I was, his middle finger dipping in and out my virgin tight ass caused my head to fall back into his shoulder. Remi's voice and reassurance that he wasn't going to hurt me quelled the anxiety.

"Maze, we don't have to if you don't want to. We don't have to go any further," he consoled. With Ezra still inside me, I had a conversation with Remi like he wasn't there.

"Are you going to be gentle Daddy?" I asked.

"Of course, baby. I don't want to hurt you. If it's too uncomfortable, invoke your safe word, we'll stop, clean up and talk it through." What I loved about Remi was it was never about him. It was always for my pleasure. He'd shut everything down if it didn't please me. In this lifestyle, consent is key. Communication is everything and Remi didn't slack at all in that way. We discussed everything. Sometimes before, sometimes dead in the middle of the act like this instance and always after the fact. Remi didn't care.

126

My safety and satisfaction were paramount. I granted him consent to enter me from behind but first, he walked Ezra through it.

"It's going to be painful to her at first until I get it in there. Hold steady until I do. Once it's in there we'll take it slow," he instructed. Ezra was a good listener and an even better learner. He held me tight, opening my cheeks, and talked to me while Remi eased his dick in my ass coaxing it open with just the head. I winced in pain but allowed him the space to do what was necessary. I listened to both him and Ezra talk me through it.

"You doin' so good baby. Remember your breathing. It's almost in there," said Remi. The pain was sharp and almost intolerable at first but once I was able to fully relax and felt the whole thing slide in easily, I let out the biggest wail and let all my nervousness go.

"Oooooh my God," I moaned. The both of them were deep inside me filling me with immaculate dick. They stood there together with me sandwiched in between slow stroking my holes. The enormous level of energy surging through my body was terrifying but mighty. I held onto Ezra's neck tight while he supported me for the both of them. Every expletive known in the English language spewed from my lips. While Ezra held me up, moaning as he fucked me, Remi reached around and rubbed my clit. It was an alarming harmony – order and anarchy with every fell of their strokes. I told them both I was about to cum. Their strokes, still in unison, intensified. I could feel the pulses in both holes. They rubbed against my spots until I squirted so hard and so much that I could have watered a lawn. My orgasm must have persuaded Remi's to arrive shortly after because I felt his arms wrap around me and his head rest against my back as he gave one last hard stroke and an oozing moan slipped from his chest.

When he was finished releasing, he slowly pulled out, grabbed a towel on the chair next to the bed, wiped his face, threw it over his shoulder and headed to the shower, leaving Ezra and I alone. Ezra turned toward the bed, placing me on my back and proceeded to fuck me stupid. I held my legs back for him and saw his soul leak from his eyes. I grinned while he stroked me. At that point, I had so much power coursing through me, I could have lit up a small village.

"Cum Ezra," I demanded. He balled up his fists on the

mattress to give himself ample support and drilled my pussy like he was mining for diamonds in it. His voice weakened to a soft tremble.

"Where?" he asked.

"Right here," I said as I pointed to my lips, licking them afterwards. My eyes never broke their gaze into his. I reached up and grabbed his face in my hand again.

"Ezra...I said...cum." I whispered. He was fading with each thrust. It didn't take him long afterwards to reach his peak.

"Oh God!" he squealed. "I'm about to nut. Oh fuck! Oh fuck!" he cussed his way through his entire flow as he jerked his dick over me. He didn't make it to my mouth which was probably for the best, but my stomach got all that work. We both laid there panting as Remi came out of the bathroom with a towel wrapped around his waist; water still dripping on him.

"Maze, the shower is still on. I'm not through with you yet," he ordered, taking Ezra's belt from around my neck. "Clean up and get back in the bed" he continued.

"Yes Sir," I obeyed. I glanced at Ezra panting on the bed and snickered. As I walked away, with Ezra's explosion dripping down my stomach, I heard him ragging on Remi.

"There's more?! Listen...my guy..." His voice became faint as I stepped into the shower to clean myself. Both holes were obnoxiously sore from both being penetrated together. The soap was a welcomed softness drizzling down my skin. I rested my head on the shower wall as I exhaled and collected my thoughts. What just happened? Did I really just fuck my man and his best friend in a threesome, and he didn't bat an eye? I couldn't believe what had just transpired in that bedroom. And it wasn't even over? What in the world could top that?!

"Now that we've gotten that out of the way, you've got to reconcile with this belt," said Remi as I came out of the shower. Ezra was then sitting back in the chair observing what it was like to be Remi. I immediately got on my hands and knees as he prepared to wear me out with the same belt that was just around my neck.

"Since I couldn't get a good spanking in while it was around your neck, we're making up for it with a more direct approach," he said calmly as he brushed the belt through his hand a few times. Excitement filled my soul as I crouched down lower to give my ass a perfect arch to play target practice with. Every strike wrapped his love around me tighter and tighter until I could no longer move. When the stars were twinkling in my eyes and the onset of subspace began kicking in, Remi gently guided my body to lay down so that could rest. I couldn't feel the sting until I started coming out of my trance hours later. When I came to, I sat up, walked to the mirror, and admired the work of art I had become. Though in remarkable pain, I was fully content and satisfied. There's no way I could ever leave Remi.

CHAPTER 9
The Phoenix

"You alive?" asked Mo through text. I smiled at my phone as I sat on the terrace soaking up the sun. My skin was still tender from the welts so the silk robe draping my skin was pacifying. I responded to Mo's text letting her know I was alright, but I had to tell her of all the anarchy that happened the night be for. As I pressed send, Remi joined me with his morning coffee in hand. He sat it on the table and lifted my robe to examine the marks on my thighs.

"How do you feel?" he asked.

"I'm ok, Daddy."

"These are terrible, baby. I'm sorry."

"Are you kidding? I love them," I assured. A look of re-morse sank on his face. In his mind, I believe he felt I was too delicate and precious to be marked up and bruised so intensely but I lived for it. The pain gave me such peace and comfort. In some dark, twisted way, the welts and bruises were signs that Remi was deep in love with me. In growing in the lifestyle, I learned that it's about safety and trust first. We were both trusting each other with our lives when we decided to embark on this journey together. It takes an enormous amount of faith in a person to allow them to inflict pain on you and an even larger amount to be allowed to do the inflicting. To the outside world, there is a thin line between what we do and physical abuse. If one isn't careful, they could find themselves in a hell storm of trouble. So, by my logic, Remi not only loved me but trusted me to no end. Yet he still felt guilt in his spirit.

"Nah baby this is too far. They should have gone down by now. Look, I broke skin right here," he surveyed, tracing my arm. My eyes followed his touch to see remnants of dried blood.

"I hadn't even noticed," I smiled. All he could do was shake his head and chuckle before sitting opposite of me.

"What are you going to do with the day, baby?" he asked. I really hadn't made any plans other than to crash on Mo's couch and run my mouth all afternoon so there wasn't much to tell him. While we sat on the terrace taking in the view, I began to think about why I hadn't been collared yet. I felt like that was the only thing missing from our experience. What was the hold up? I know he had to know it's what I wanted. As I was thinking, my face snitched on me and told Remi I was lost in reflection.

"What's on your mind, baby?"

"Nothing. Why?" I murmured. In attempt to deflect, I continued. "Beautiful day, it'nit?"

Remi wasn't buying it for one cent.

"Mandisa, what's the matter?" His voice became stern and authoritative. I swallowed the lump in my throat like bitter medicine. I loved and hated the way he knew me so well. Sighing heavily, I went ahead and bit the bullet inquiring about a collar.

"Sir...I'm wondering why you haven't collared me yet. We've been together living in this dynamic for months now. It's clear neither of us are leaving the relationship. Why haven't we made this official?"

My voice trembled slightly as I aired my grievances to him. His eyes didn't shift from mine, yet mine lowered in humility. I could never look him directly in his eyes in fear of sudden weakness. It had always been hard for me to speak about what I was feeling because of past relationship traumas. Openly, sometimes I was afraid to ask him for the things I wanted and needed because of rejection issues. Remi, however, never allowed that to be an excuse for not talking to him. The silence between us was uncomfortable while he processed what I had just said to him.

"Maze, I honestly didn't know it meant that much to you, baby. I'm still new to this whole Dom thing; still learning the ins and outs. Grant me patience. You know you can have whatever you want from me. I'm sorry I didn't treat this matter with the urgency you needed me to," he explained. My heart felt lighter in hearing those words come from his mouth. It was that easy with him. There was relief in my smile as he rose from the table to kiss me. Lifting my head by my chin, he bit my bottom lip.

"You know you're my favorite little thing, Maze. We'll talk about this collar later. I have to make a run before work," he promised. He kissed my forehead and chuckled as he waded the doorway.

"I think we fucked Ezra's head up, too. I have to check on him and make sure he aight," he added. I burst into laughter.

"Yea Daddy, that was insane. Are you ok?" I asked. He became still in the doorway with no hesitation.

"Hell yea I'm ok. Are you ok?! Yo' ass got handed to you last night. Literally!" Heavy laughter erupted between the both of us as we briefly joked about the rogueries that transpired with his friend. Before going back inside, he winked at me and told me he would check in on me later. I said 'ok' and turned my head back toward the city to take it in a short while longer before preparing to spend the day with Mo.

Remi

     Ezra was already at Rasa in his office when I got there. I
knocked on the door before entering. Before I could get a word in
edgewise, Ezra put his file down and looked at me with widened
eyes.
     "Breh..."
     "You good?"
     "The fuck you mean?! That shit was crazy! I mean...I
enjoyed it thoroughly, and and and...I won't mind joining in again
but...that shit was crazy, mang! Ya'll get down like that all the
time?!" His curiosity began to run wild.
     "That was the first time doing anything like that but yea,
shit gets pretty wild with her, bruh," I explained.
     "That didn't make you feel a kind of way? Dawg, I fucked
ya' girl. Ain't that against code or something?" he nervously asked.
I couldn't help but laugh, leaning up against the doorpost.
     "Nah man, we good. She just free like that and I be wit' the
shit she on," I said, shrugging my shoulders.
     "Aight well...I aint nut in her or anything like that so..." he
assured me. His face was almost begging for permission to if there
just so happened to be a "next time" between us. I didn't give it to
him when I pushed off the doorpost and went to my office.
     "Yea aight. Better not had," I said, walking away. The trip
to my office was a bit longer than usual. There was a slight draft
in the hallway and the smell of barbecue filled my nose from the
kitchen as the house chef was preparing for our guests. Digging
in my pockets for my keys, I was confused to see my office door
already cracked open. I looked around baffled because no one was
scheduled until later except for my kitchen team, Ezra, and me.
There were sounds of rummaging happening, so I slowly pushed
the door open, peering in before I walked through. I became instantly annoyed as the mysterious shuffler became visible.
     "Fire, what you doin' in here? You not scheduled to work
until later. How you even get into my office?" I probed.
     "I let myself in. Your cleaning crew does a shit job at keep-
ing the master keys locked up," she grinned, spinning the large set

of keys around her finger. I already had to convince Maze I wasn't fuckin' her and there she was making it painfully obvious that I was.

"Fire, I told you we can't get down like that anymore. I already had to let Leilani go because she got out of line. I ain't got not one problem getting you up out of here either," I growled. My resistance seemed to turn her on even more as she switched towards me.

"Oh right. You got a new girl. How's that going for you?" she inquired.

"Great, actually, so I'ma need you to get the fuck up outta here until your shift starts, Fire. I mean it." She was persistent in trying to seduce me, using her big ass tits and curvy hips to reel me in.

"I bet her pussy don't grip like mine do though. And why did you break up with Leilani, anyway? We always had so much fun together, remember?" she coaxed, pressing her body against mine. Her hands began to cruise over my arms. Visions of our 3-sums dashed across my mind. Her pussy was always bomb. That's why I started calling her 'Fire'. The way her short ass took dick always thrilled me. Even after Leilani and I split, I kept fucking her and continued our tumultuous relationship until Maze and I made our relationship exclusive. She wasn't too happy about it and always made it clear when Maze came to the club. Even though I sexed her a few more times during me and Maze's relationship, she was never going to be my girl and she knew it, so she went out of her way to drop hints to Maze. I was glad my dick could blind her intuition because she was spot on when she called me out on it that night she called herself leaving. I ended things with Fire that night when I got to the club, but it didn't stop her from trying me.

Coming back to my senses, I backed Fire away from me and told her to get out of my office before I terminated her. She kissed her teeth, rolled her eyes, and stormed out, slamming my office door. I sat in my chair and composed myself. I just couldn't fuck things up with Maze. She became a lifeline. There wasn't a pussy walking the planet worth losing her. She gave me something women like Fire and Leilani never could. She built my confidence. She became my safe haven. Maze was proof that God existed, and He so loved me that He plucked out a feather from His right wing, named her Mandisa and let her float right into my hands.

While I sat there, I began thinking about this collar business Maze was so unyielding about. If I was honest with myself, I didn't understand the big deal until I did a little recon. I learned the symbolism and importance in having one. My heart suddenly sank, and everything became clear: Maze just wanted to solidify our relationship. She wanted to be bonded to me in her submission. But we were already tethered in every way. We didn't need a piece of leather to consecrate what we had just like a piece of paper wouldn't make us any more married to each other. But for Maze: anything. As I looked for different ideas, Ezra, came into my office, looking around confused.

"Yo, why Fire just stomp passed me like she ready to fight? She tryna give you pussy again?" he questioned. I didn't take my eyes off my laptop while scrolling.

"Yea man. She betta get her ass outta here," I downplayed. Ezra knew we used to fuck around but he was under the impression that when Leilani and I split, so did she and I. Fire was good at keeping a secret or so I thought. I kept scrolling intently as Ezra took notice.

"Breh, what are you looking for?" he prodded, sitting on my desk.

"Maze been askin' me to collar her for the longest and I just brushed it off until this morning when she looked like she was about to cry asking me about it again," I explained.

"A collar?! Like…those things cats, dogs and small monkeys wear?" he joked.

"Ayo shut up! But yea. Somethin' like that. I didn't grasp the concept or importance of it until this morning. Bro, she was upset trying to explain to me why she should be collared. She sat there like 'haven't I been a good girl? Aren't I deserving of the honor?' and I just sat there blinking. What was I supposed to say to that other than 'you're right baby. I'll get you a collar today'?

"So, what you gon' do? That sounds…permanent."

"I mean…it kind of is. To subs, being collared is almost equivalent to being married and in some cases it is, so…" Ezra stared in bafflement as I continued.

"If I'ma do this, I have to come correct," I ended. Looking through ideas for collars, nothing seemed to jump out at me, so I pulled my phone from off my hip.

"Who you callin'?" asked Ezra.

"My jeweler."

"Bougie ass muh'fucka. Can't never just go to the mall like normal people,"

"Nope," I snipped. Ezra stood up and walked out.

"Whatever. Stay toxic, my guy," he sneered. As the sound of his footsteps down the hall became distant, my jeweler picked up.

"Aye, Stone, it's Jeremiah. What's going on? Yea, yea I'm chillin'. I need you to come through. I have an idea I need you for. Like an hour? Yea I'll be here. Aight cool. See you then. Thanks, my friend."

Once off the phone with my jeweler, I texted Maze and told her to meet me at the club because there were people coming, I wanted her to meet. Reading "yes Daddy" in response to my request made my dick hard. I knew I didn't want anything like a standard collar. The leather straps were cool, but Maze deserved to be draped in diamonds. My plan was to see if my jeweler could merge the two before Maze got there.

When he arrived, it was like the President had walked into my office. His security detail was off the charts. Two stationed outside my door, one at the top of the stairwell, two guarding the front entrance, two at the back and a special ops team in my lobby. He was the best jeweler in town, so anybody with money knew who he was. They knew if he had even a briefcase with him, there was likely a million dollars' worth of jewels in it, at least. Walking into Rasa, not only did he carry a briefcase, but he also hauled an entire trunk with him which he followed behind in precession; one of his guards pushing it ahead of him.

Stone was an averaged height, balding African man that wore glasses that hung off his flared nostrils. He was elderly so he moved with his three daughters behind him. They were more his bodyguards than the full team of gorillas shielding my doors. He entered my office with the regality of Obatala. I held my hand out to shake his.

"Baba! What a long time it's been, my friend. You're still looking good," I cheered.

"Jeremiah, young king. You flatter me. You remember my

138

daughters, yes?" he presented. They were emotionless as they stood behind him; tall, mighty, and damned sexy. Every time I saw Stone, he would try to arrange a marriage between me and one of them not knowing I used to secretly have a thing going on with his oldest.

"Yes, I remember. Hello, ladies. It's a pleasure," I greeted. They remained silent, though all with a twinkle of yearning in their eyes. I caught eyes with my old flame and for a second, I could have sworn it looked as if she was melting right where she stood. As Stone, slammed his briefcase on my desk, she was startled back into her stance. I smiled and turned my focus towards him. His wrinkled hands trembled as he turned the dial on the combination lock. As he opened the panels, the sparkle was almost blinding. He brought rings, bracelets, anklets, and other types of jewelry all encased in precious metals and gems.

What I was looking for was a necklace. I perused through the wall of jewels and came across a choker that looked like a strap fully wrapped in diamonds. It looked as if it would pass as a collar, so I picked it up and weighed it with my hand. I was rather weighty, which I liked. When Stone noticed I took an interest in that piece, he handed me his loupe to examine the detail and clarity of the small crystals. He was always so proud of his work; not a rock was uneven or out of place. I fell in love with it instantly. I turned towards him, choker still in hand, with an unusual request.

"Can you add an O ring to this?" I asked. A look of shock and confusion waved over Stone's face, but he was willing to accommodate my wish. Along with the choker, I wanted a neck-lace Maze could wear daily and treat it as a collar as well. Wearing the one I had in my hand would bring too much attention, but I knew her official collar had to be extravagant. I asked Stone to see his individual jewels to which he then unlocked his trunk. I had never seen so much money in such a small piece of luggage. He had rocks the sizes of grains of sand all the way to small boulders. There were diamonds, emeralds, sapphires, and other rare gems but what caught my eye was a teardrop shaped ruby that was big enough to be noticed but small enough to not draw any unwanted attention to it.

"Stone, set this one for me," I pointed.

"Excellent choice, my son. For a ring?" he asked. I didn't

take my eyes off it.

"No, a necklace. Can you have it back here by seven o'clock?"

"For you, my boy, no problem," he assured. He handed me the bill and I walked over to my safe to pay it. As I grabbed the stacks, he cased up the choker and secured the ruby to take back with him. He walked over to me where we exchanged money and farewells. Shaking Stone's hand once again, he thanked me for my business and guaranteed me he'll have the pieces delivered by seven. He and his basket of brutes along with his fine ass daughters walked out `without a trace of them ever being there. While I waited, I caught up with some paperwork and made a few phone calls to lock in potential bookings.

By six o'clock there was a knock at my office door. I told the person on the other side it was open and as a gargantuan beast opened my door, Stone's oldest daughter walked through with 2 black velvet boxes, one on top of the other, in hand.

"Bhanoyi," I smiled. I rose from my seat to properly greet her. Her slender frame stood tall hugged in a fitting royal blue maxi dress. Her blond, low fade and blue eyes set her apart from a lot of women I'd ever been with. There was never bad blood between us when we stopped dealing with each other, so the exchange was pleasant. We spent a few minutes catching up until she realized she hadn't handed me my purchase yet.

"For a girlfriend?" she asked, extended her arm.

"Yea, something like that. You've gotta meet her. You'll love her. She's into the same things you are," I suggested. I told her a little bit more about Maze watching her eyes light up.

"Really? Tell her I have questions then," she agreed. Bhanoyi was similar to Maze in that she loved being controlled, but she didn't know how to articulate it completely and effectively. Maze would love her. Bhanoyi and her sisters handled a lot of their father's business, as he was growing less capable of ripping and running which is why she delivered my necklace rather than him. As we continued to chat, I opened the first box to see the beautifully set ruby dangling from a thin white gold chain. The second box damn near blinded me upon opening it. The diamond choker with the addition of the O ring looked exactly as I imagined it. I looked up at Bhanoyi in awe.

"They're gorgeous, Jeremiah. Your girl is going to love it," she glared. Though we were no longer in regular communication, Bhanoyi and I never lost love for each other. We could have been together, but I was still playing games and she was too good a woman to mess over like that. Stone would have handed her to me with no qualms had he known we had a thing. She stood close to me, admiring the necklace alongside me. Our gaze caught each other. I could never resist her when she looked at me.

"You and those eyes. Move away from me woman." We shared a laugh as she backed away and shook her head. No one believed her eyes were naturally blue, but her late mother and both her sisters carried the same genes. Stone believed himself to be among the most blessed because of it. He would always say it was his luck in life to be blessed to have women on his arm with eyes clearer than the diamonds he sold. I agreed with him every time.

As Bhanoyi moved towards my door and said her goodbye, I walked closely behind her to escort her out. I caught a whiff of her perfume. She smelled exactly like Maze. The smell of grapefruit gently guided me back to my senses. I told her I'd be calling her soon so she could meet Maze and she smiled in agreement. We kissed each other's cheek before she walked out in front of her security. I stood in the doorway and watched her float away. Maze would fall in love with Bhanoyi, I continued to think. I plotted on setting up the meet and greet for after I collared her. Looking at my watch, I realized we were due to open shortly. I put my new purchase in my safe and headed downstairs.

Once opened, it didn't take long for the crowd to file in. The air was unusually thick that evening. I looked around and figured it was because of all the bodies dancing around and surrounding the bar. I stood atop the second-floor balcony raking the room below. I was anxious for Maze to arrive. I knew she'd be over the moon when I presented her with her collar. I was going to make her the belle of the ball when she arrived. As I stood there watching the crowd continue to fall in, Ezra noticed me and stopped in his tracks.

"You good, Boss?"

"Yea, I'm good, bro. Aye listen, I'ma be in my office for a bit. When Maze gets here, tell her to come up. I have something planned. She should be here in a few minutes."

"Aight cool. I'll let her know. Oh! Remind me to bring you up to speed on security after tonight, too," he said, running off as if he something urgently needed his attention. I peeped Fire next to us out of the side of my eye but presumed she was just doing her job. I headed back up to my office, nerves on edge. I poured myself a short drink to calm them down and went to my safe. Once cracked, I opened the box with her collar in it. Stone didn't disappoint. Anticipating the look on Maze's face when she'd see it, I hoped it'd take her breath away. As I stood there rearranging the contents of the safe, I heard the door open and close. I smiled, still facing the wall.

"Maze, baby, I'm glad you're here. I want to talk to you," I said. She didn't say a word. Her footsteps toward me were light; almost secretive like she didn't want anyone to know she was there. I felt her arms wrap underneath mine to allow her hands to rub my chest. My eyes closed as I let her caress me. Granted, it felt good, but her touch was different; not as warm. I felt kisses to my back that weren't my girl's. Turning around, to find out who the imposter hugging me was, I see Fire with the most sinister smirk on her face. I pulled her arms off me, snatching my body out from her grip.

"Fire, what the fuck, yo. Why are you here?! My girl gon' be here any second. You have to go!"

"Maze? That's what you call her?" she asked, backing me up into the wall, attempting to kiss on me.

"Yes, and if she sees you here, she gon whoop yo ass! I need you to leave," I pleaded.

"She won't," she laughed. I was trying not to beat this woman myself, but her aggressiveness was stronger than my self-restraint. She kissed on my neck and popped the top buttons off my shirt by snatching it open.

"Jeremiah, stop acting like you don't wanna fuck this good pussy again," she sneered. She took my hand and guided it under her skirt to reveal she wasn't wearing panties. Her pussy was warm and wet as fuck. I was ashamed of my dick beginning to get hard. Fire groped me only to come to the same discovery and smiled wider than the devil herself on Halloween.

"Look who missed me," she mocked. I tried my hardest to get her off me, but my strength failed me. She managed to get her

142

hands into my pants and pulled my dick out jerking it to get it hard. "What's the matter, Boss? Scared?"

"Yes. Fire you have to go! If my girl catch you here, I'm dead," I pleaded. Fire paid me no attention and attempted to lower herself to her knees and give me head. I struggled so hard trying not to hit her but if I didn't physically attack her, she would have kept going. Before she could put her mouth on me, I pushed back and slapped her so hard I fell back into the wall. No sooner than she hit the floor and held her face in shock, Maze walked through the door.

Everything froze. Maze stood there like a deer caught in the headlights trying to assess what was going on. She looked at Fire on the floor with her skirt above her waist then at me with my dick hanging out, solid as a 20-year friendship, and shirt ripped open. I could physically see all the trust she had for me leave her heart as she shook her head, trying to not cry leaving my office. I rushed to fix myself and run after her.

"Maze, baby wait! No! It's not what you think! Maze!" I exclaimed. As I bolted out of my office, still zipping my pants up, I pushed passed my head of security, Chayce, and told him to throw Fire out of the building immediately. There were so many people in the club that night. Trying to follow Maze was like blood trying to circulate through clogged arteries. I kept my eyes on her back, following her trail out of the building. I called to her, but it was so loud, she couldn't hear me. By the time I fell out of the front door and looked around, I could just see her foot climbing into a limo and it speeding off down the street. I threw my hands behind my head, screaming to keep from crying. There was still a line of people trying to get in who saw me lash out in anger, banging my hands against steel doors. Moments later, Chayce came shuffling out, with a struggling Fire in toe. Dropping her to the ground, he dusted his hands off and looked around.

"Which one of ya'll is next? Mind your business," he roared. The waiting party goers quickly turned their heads. As I paced the immediate sidewalk, Fire stumbled to get up. There was no shame or repentance in her heart. She laughed, pulling down her skirt and adjusting her top. Her curly, brown hair was disheveled and her face glowed red with my handprint.

"I'll see you in court then?" she said. I lunged at her again,

143

but Chayce and 2 other security guards restrained me.

"Fire, get your ass outta here before I fuck you up!" I screamed. It was the first time I had ever lost control that way. I could have killed that bitch. Once she was off my property, I rushed to contact Maze. I called her phone back-to-back for an hour straight with no answer. I was about to leave the club and pull up on her, but she turned her location off. My palms became sweaty, and my lungs began to close. My chest was tight with a pain I had never experienced. It had to have been literal heartbreak. When her phone went to voicemail after I called again, I became so frustrated, I trashed my entire office. Ezra walked into the outrage. I stumbled back and fell to the floor, bawling. He rushed to my aide.

"Whoa whoa! What happened?!" he questioned. In between sobs and gasps for air, I explained what happened to the best of my ability and told him that Maze wasn't answering my calls. He held onto me for a few minutes to help me regain my composure. The music was so loud downstairs. No one knew of the chaos that was unfolding in my office. When I became calm enough to function, I stared into the floor I had collapsed on.

"I was going to collar her tonight, Ez," I confided. I showed him the jewelry and rested my head on the wall. Ezra did what any good friend would do, trying to stay positive.

"She knows you'd kill for her, Boss. Give her some space. She'll come around," he comforted.

"Nah, Ez. She already thought me, and Fire were fuckin'. I got her to relax about it and now it's like her suspicions were true. Breh, my whole dick was hard and that bitch whole pussy was out. There's no way I can convince Maze she aint see what she saw. I can't even try to explain that," I stammered. Ezra just sat there quietly and gave me space to think. I couldn't move. I kept reimagining the look on her face over and over when she walked in. That was years of a strong bond, broken in an instant. If I'd lost her for good, I wasn't sure I'd be able to recover. By time I got off the floor, the club was closed, and the last patron stumbling out. I called Maze once more before heading downstairs.

"Heeey, you've reached Mandi. I..."

I hung up the phone before her voicemail told me she couldn't answer. I was like a zombie going down the stairs. My bartenders, bottle girls and hosts were counting cash with Ezra before closing out. He peeped me walking to the door in a daze and made sure no one bothered me on my way out. Everything seemed so much bigger than me in that moment. It felt like I had to climb into my truck and slump down to press the gas. The air surrounding me was suffocating like I was a million miles under the sea. The street-lights glared into my eyes; everything was blurry. My probable reality came to the forefront: I was likely going to lose Maze. We had already discussed what cheating was, what it looked like and set our boundaries early in our relationship. Added with the fact that she already had her uncertainties about my dealings with Fire, I knew it was over after seeing what she saw. There was no excuse nor any getting around it. I just couldn't help calling one last time, though.

"Heeey, you've reached Mandi. I..."

Mandisa

I took a week off from the magazine, collected myself
in the process and returned to work as usual. I blocked out any
thoughts of Remi since I found him with his dick practically
thumping that bitch's forehead. I knew he was fucking her. He
went through all that trouble to convince me he wasn't, but my
gut was never wrong. I knew I should have trusted it. I blocked
his number after the hundredth time he called me that night and
didn't think twice about it. I cried profusely for the first two day
afterwards but on the third day, I rose without a care like I was the
reason the world celebrated Easter.

Walking into the office, the air was cleaner than usual.
Trinnie must have called a contractor while I was away and had
them change the filters. It just seems a lot easier to breathe. The
high ceilings and metal beams felt like I was walking through the
industrial part of Heaven. I missed seeing the huge pictures of our
covers adorning the walls. I was generally in a very good mood on
my first day back to work after having my heart trampled on.

The bop in my step had my entire staff confused and
nervous. They stared at me as if I were a ticking time bomb but to
assure them that I was ok, I smiled gracefully and said hi to everyone who made eye contact with me. My office was at the very
end of the long hall in the middle edge of the building. The walk
became awkward with everyone's necks turning. It started to feel
like a walk of shame down a Roman street where I was going to
be stoned in front of the entire town. Even Trinnie's face was to
the floor as I strutted passed her. What was everybody staring at?
I was ok! As I reached my office door, I opened it with confidence
and stormed in only to be met with a week's worth of flowers,
chocolates, and other gifts from Remi with notes attached to them
that begged me to 'just talk' to him. See it all caused a sharp pain
in my stomach and a twitch in my eye. A loud, long, and desperate
scream vaulted from my belly. I turned back around with fury in
my face to see everyone, including Trinnie gathered in the middle
of the hall, frozen with their mouths collapsing to the floor one by
one, staring into my office. I slammed the door and hauled each

146

vase at the walls. My stiletto heels were used to crush the boxes of chocolates and I didn't even bother reading the notes passed the first one.

When there was no more havoc to wreak, I exhaled, pulled my hair back behind my ears, stepped over all the glass and walked out like nothing happened. After fixing my clothes, my head lifted itself and my heart gave my legs just enough strength to exit the building and go back home. As I was making my way back down the hall, my staff scrambled around me as if their jobs were about to be demolished like the flowers I left on the floor. I didn't even bother closing my door. Let the world see all the destruction left in my wake and have it served as a warning. Besides, I had a cleaning crew that would take my office back to its pristine order before the end of day.

My phone alerted me to a text the second I closed my car door. It was Trinnie apologizing saying she should have warned me before I got there. Her saving grace was she didn't know I was coming back to work that day and by time she realized it was me, it was too late. Although my anger was not directed towards her, I didn't respond to the message. I just wanted to get back home.

I refused to let this be the same as with Aziz: depressed for months, not caring what I looked like, borderline alcoholic…I couldn't go back to that space. I had to keep myself occupied; act like Remi never existed. Before heading home, I made a pit stop at my local beauty supply store to get hair bleach, a color rinse, and a brand-new lip color; one I'd never been bold enough to wear. While I could have simply made an appointment with my hair stylist, this process had to be all me.

The washed linen smell from the newly changed freshener tickled my nose as I entered my condo. Fortunately, I had enough composure and common sense to not destroy my place of refuge because of my hurt. I didn't hesitate in changing the locks the day after I left Remi. He was never the type to disrespect me by just popping up anyway, but I just did not want to leave room for him trying to lie his way back into my space. Deadbolting the door, I fumbled through my mail then tossed it on the receiving table once I saw there was nothing of importance in it.

I went to my room to take my work clothes off and change into something I didn't mind getting messed up because of the dye and rinse. Reading through the instructions, I heaved a big sigh, looked myself in the mirror and hyped myself up before I talked myself out of shitting on the world.

Once all the dye was in my hair and processing, I placed a shower cap over my head and let it do its thing. I sat on my bed, grabbing my laptop. I was surfing the internet until the sudden urge to book a trip hit me. I hadn't been on one in a while, and it was probably just what the doctor would order had I gone to see one. It didn't take much to talk myself into it, so I started looking up destinations. Nowhere in the U.S could heal a broken heart. Jamaica was too cliché for a situation like mine and I've been to most of the other Caribbean Islands several times as well. It was time to look abroad. London, Paris, Kenya, South Africa, Tokyo; all places that didn't call to me. I wasn't going to get my groove back or connect to my roots and come back overly 'woke'. I just needed a place where I could dip off to, decompress and nurse my broken heart a bit.

After a bit more internet surfing, Tahiti popped up on my radar. It wasn't a bad idea. I looked up flights and a hotel, booking the trip for the next day. Once my trip was confirmed, I texted Trinnie and Mo in our group chat telling them I'd be back in 10 days. Neither of them asked questions, simply responding with 'ok boo' and 'travel safely. Don't get pregnant.'

By the time I got my confirmation emails and my airline app alerted me to my flight status, it was time for me to wash the dye out of my hair. The blonde didn't look bad on me, but I needed something bolder. I needed to attract attention. Saturating my bleached hair with the semi-permanent color seemed easy enough. Placing another cap over my head, I went to pack my bags. Because I'd be gone for 10 days, I knew it had to be at least a month's worth of clothes and shoes to pack. My big body suitcase was buried in my coat closet up front and I had to move things around to get to it.

I pulled every piece of white clothing I owned off the closet rack. This was going to be a cleansing voyage for me. Just as I became confident that I was set with enough clothing, I took notice to a little black dress I had been dying to wear. I stood there debating on whether or not I should drizzle this little bit of molasses over all the sugar in my suitcase. I quickly snatched it from the hanger and tossed it in with everything else before I changed my mind.

When I was all packed, I rinsed the color out of my hair. Although the water never ran clear, I was positive the 3 washes and 4 rinses removed all the residual color from my strands. The second I looked into the mirror, everything around my turned grey. The only color I saw was the ruby red of my tresses. I loved it. It was everything I was going for. 'Sexy' was an understatement for what it made me feel. I became the girl with hair like fire. I set my hair in rollers and allowed it to dry overnight. My villain origin story began with the drop of my last curl the next morning before I left out for my flight. It was over for men. I was out for blood. Clearly, they couldn't handle a woman who enjoyed being submissive. They wanted to be stepped on and it was evident in the way they moved around me. Remi, Aziz…both lessons in how I needed to be to dominate one. I carried their souls around my neck as trophies, walking out of my door leaving to catch my flight. The takeaway from my relationships with them was the fact that I knew I was the best thing to happen to them in life and it made them both sick to know I was living and thriving without them.

Remi

Maze really left me without letting me explain what truly happened that night. How could she after the bond we built?
After all the intimate moments, the vulnerability we both showed.
I opened my chest wide for this woman just for her to snatch my
heart and walk away with it still beating in her hand. I was sick as
a dog to my stomach knowing she was out there living life without
me. I cried every day for a month straight. Taking time off from
Rasa and letting Ezra run the show, I stayed couped up in my room
aching for Maze's body next to mine. It had been just about a
month since she walked away and two weeks since I locked myself
in my house, short of chaining myself to the bedpost in protest. I
don't even think I washed my balls within that timeframe because
there was no point to do so, in my mind. Never had I been through
such withdrawals from a woman.

Though it was mid-afternoon, my room was pitch black because I ordered my housekeeper to keep my curtains closed and to
stay out of my room. My chef knocked on my door several times a
day leaving food and snacks for me to eat. I only went for it when
my stomach knocked on my back. I was down bad. There was no
consoling me. I was completely devastated from Mandisa leaving.

One morning, Ezra came to the house to find me still in my
room fast asleep. He yanked the curtains back and started yelling
throughout the entire room.

"Bro, get'cho depressed ass up! It's been two weeks! You
need to eat; you need to shower 'cause you stink and you need to
pull yourself together!" he chastised. I jumped up, squinting my
eyes as the sunlight threw fire into them.

"How did you get in here?" I grumbled.

"Your housekeeper let me in. Get up, I said! Enough is a
god damn nough! She aint comin' back! It's time to move on," he
bullied. I reason that he saw the despair all over me as he ceased
attacking me, sighed and came to sit on the bed.

"She meant that much, huh?"

"Means, Ezra. She means that much. I can't believe she
would do this to me," I divulged.

"Well, homie...look at what happened. She was supposed to leave. You fucked up."

"You're not helping. Besides...I didn't do anything. That bitch came onto me. I just wish I had a way to prove that to Maze. Ezra, I need her," I sobbed. Ezra just sat there quietly in deep thought. After several minutes of quietness, he stood up and started gathering the clothes I had sprawled all over the room and putting them in a pile outside my door for the housekeeper.

"Look, I have to go. We've several parties booked tonight. You need to get the fuck up. I'ma give you until the weekend to sulk and mope around here. Come Monday, you gettin' up. At least wash ya' nuts before then though. I can smell you from here. Ah god!" he exclaimed, slamming my door. He yelled to my chef to make me a bologna and cheese sandwich as he left. Hearing his obnoxious engine rev up and peel out of my driveway, I rolled over and stared out of the window. He was right. I had to get up. I just didn't have the strength to. All I could think of was Maze. Where was she? What was she doing? Was she thinking about me? As I laid there, the urge to pee struck me and the reminder to wash my nuts played again in my head. I pulled my pajama pants open and caught a whiff of that situation and damn near killed myself from the stench. It wasn't right. I had to get it together. But how?

CHAPTER 10
The Phoenix

Mandisa

Tahiti was everything I needed it to be: relaxation, good food, gorgeous men, sand in my toes, sunrays kissing my skin evenly; it was incredible. I didn't want to come back to the States. Thirteen-hour flights seem like only two when you aren't trying to leave a place. Once landed, I exited the plane and returned to the smoggy, polluted, Jersey air smell. I immediately groaned in despair. This couldn't be real life.

The other passengers were rude and angry, jockeying for position to get out of the airport as fast as they could. I managed to get to baggage claim without being trampled or having to fight someone, patiently waiting for my suitcase to come around. The trip to public transportation was short and sweet with taxis lined up and Ubers not too far away. Luckily, I didn't have to rely on either service as Gio was already there waiting for me. He had another gentleman with him who carried my luggage to the limo. I kissed Gio on both cheeks as usual as he held his arm out for me to take.

I looked important being escorted to a black suburban parked in the taxi lane. I had my newly colored hair in a high ponytail, expensive shades that rested on my face delicately and my outfit lent itself perfectly fitting. Giovanni and his other driver ushered me to my condo where there was no one to welcome me home.

Kicking my sandals off before I could get to the door, I unlocked it and allowed the sweet-smelling air to lay itself over me like a thin sheet of roses and lilies. I couldn't undress fast enough. While I didn't want to be back in the States, I was happy to be home. As I unpacked my carryon bag, I realized that I never took my phone off airplane mode. I tapped the blue switch and once my phone caught a good signal, alert after alert started coming through. Placing the phone on the dresser, it beeped uncontrollably for close to 30 seconds more. Once it stopped, I began to check what was causing all the ruckus before I texted the girls to let them know I was home:

Email.
Email.
Text from a subscription service
Email
DM from a low life
Email
Text from an unknown number...

My heart sank immediately. Most of my soul said don't even read it. However, facing my fears, I tapped on the bolded conversation, eyes widening when I found out who it was.

"Maze, this is Ezra. We need to meet as soon as possible."

The room fell silent. I couldn't hear anything but my heart pounding out of my chest. What could he possibly want? Did something happen to Remi? Was he trying to shoot his shot? I battled back and forth with myself as to whether I should respond but in knowing myself, I wouldn't be able to rest until I uncovered what his reason for contacting me was.

"Where?" I replied. It took him 20 minutes to get back to me. I sat on my bed biting my nails until my phone pinged.

"Saga on Halsey. 3 o'clock."

The hanging clock on the wall mocked me as I looked at the time and scoffed in between panicking, considering it was only a half an hour from then. My face hadn't rubbed off during my flight, so I rejoiced in it being one less thing I had to do before running back out of the house. A change of attire was necessary as I wasn't about to go meet my ex's boy looking like a bum. I let my hair down and fluffed up what little curl I still had and headed out the door.

The entire drive over was mentally hectic. It was the longest seven minutes I'd ever driven through. My nerves failed me as every last one of them began a wave in my body and an unnerving started to set in. I had to turn the AC on and fan myself at the same time because of the anxiety. Every single red light seemed to catch

155

me and everyone else on the road drove slower than sap running down a tree in winter. Unusually, it was fairly easy to find a parking spot that day. That area of town is regularly filled with patrons. Before getting out of the car, I took a deep breath to collect myself.

When I walked up, Ezra was already seated and sipping a Stella. I swept my hair to the side so that it could drape my exposed shoulder and continued my walk to the table. He stood and smiled, greeting me with a kiss to the cheek. I returned the embrace and allowed him to pull my chair out for me. My heart wasn't prepared for anything he was going to say but I made space to receive it.

"You look incredible, Maze," he began.

"Thank you, Ezra," I acknowledged before cutting right to the chase. "Why am I here?" Ezra was lost for words briefly because he was never used to a woman being so cutthroat and to the point. My face remained as straight as a sinner who caught a sneak peek of hell and was sent back to Earth. Once gathered, his words came back to him.

"Look, I don't want to waste time. Jeremiah is fading. He's doing bad Maze. He needs you." My poker face remained undefeated.

"That sounds like a him problem, Ezra. I wasn't the one who cheated."

"Neither was he," he barked. Anger and frustration filled his voice. The audacity of this man to try and refute what my eyes saw. I felt all the rage I had suppressed so well begin to bubble up.

"Ezra, you brought me here for this?"

"No. I brought you here to ask you to stop being a bitch for two seconds and give me the grace you didn't give Jeremiah and just listen," he snapped. I clutched my invisible pearls as the rebuttal was swatted down before it could even fly off the table. His tone remained low as to not cause a scene.

"I know you think he cheated on you, but he didn't. The girl came onto him, and he tried to block her at every turn, but she was just doing too much. When she pulled his dick out and tried to go down on him, he slapped her and that's when you walked in," he explained. I was outraged. How could he pass that bullshit story off to me and expect me to not only believe it but go running back to Jeremiah. As I was expressing my frustration, Ezra was fum-

156

bling through his phone.

"Really?! First, you make up this cockamamie story on behalf of your boy then you don't even respect me enough to listen when I speak. Look, I'm sorry to interrupt what I'm sure was a well thought out story but what I saw with my own eyes outweighs the story you're trying to spin. Jeremiah lied and cheated. Point blank period and I'm over it. So, if you'll excuse me, I'm done being lied to," I snapped. Just as I was getting up, Ezra tossed his phone onto the table.

"Sit down, Mandisa. There's something you need to see," he asserted. I looked at him with a hint of curiosity while his expression remained uncompromising. I slowly lowered back into the chair, picking up his phone. My stomach turned in knots with anxiety. The more I watched, I realized it was security footage from that night, my mouth dropped. It was exactly as Ezra described it. The woman did come on to him and he tried to push her away. I saw every angle that supported his narrative, but I still couldn't believe it.

"This doesn't prove anything, Ezra. He was probably pushing her away because of the cameras," I argued.

"He didn't know the cameras were there, Mandisa. I just had them installed. I was going to tell him about it after the night was over but then everything went to shit. I didn't even know they had already started recording until I had to run footage back for an attempted burglary at the club last week. The police wanted to check for possible clues and prior evidence, and it went all the way to the beginning of that day," he disclosed. His seriousness turned into a plea for help.

"Go to him Mandisa. He didn't cheat on you. Sure, it looked like he didn't do too much to stop her, but it was because he didn't want to catch an assault charge. That man is withering away without you," he appealed. I sat with my thoughts briefly as the waitress came back to the table asking if I would like anything. I politely waved 'no thank you' and continued to ponder. I felt like a fool. I didn't give Remi the benefit of the doubt. I just took what I saw for face value and bolted. In my defense, I was triggered from previous experience. I wasn't going to put up with it with Remi just as I didn't with Aziz. As I deliberated in my head, Ezra commenced to graveling again.

"Please Maze. Go see about him. He isn't eating, he isn't exercising, and he stinks. He hasn't washed his ass in God knows how long," he implored.

"Damn, that bad?"

"That man is completely bonkers over this, Maze," he affirmed. I dwelled in conviction. What felt like hours, happened to only be five minutes that went by in real time while I weighed out my options. I could either not go and leave the entire relationship in the trash or I could show up and fix things with the man I was excruciatingly in love with. If I went back, I could put myself at risk of potentially being hurt again. I didn't want that. But I had to stop being dishonest with myself and acknowledge that Remi was undoubtedly the love of my life and that life was so much better with him. As Ezra finished his beer, I rose from the table; head held high.

"I'm sorry, I can't Ezra," I lied. He shook his head and dropped it in disappointment. I was letting him down, but I just couldn't muster up the courage to face Remi even though I did nothing wrong. He was my only weakness. I knew if I saw him, I'd forget the pain that was caused. I left money on the table for his drink and walked away without looking back. Fighting tears, I made my way back to the car.

The ride home with long and torturesome. An unbearable pain lodged itself in my chest. We vowed never to do this to each other. Our promise was "Always Us". We said we would always choose each other over everything else yet I was leaving him to suffer alone. The fear of being misled somehow always seemed to overshadow what was right in front of my eyes. If I had to look deeper, Remi would never hurt a fly. He was a gorgeous man so I had to accept that women would flock to him always but hurting me was not something he went out his way to do. To boot, I realized that I was not giving myself enough credit in this situation either. I was unforgettable; my submission was my superpower and although I didn't weaponize it, I knew I could use it to obtain whatever it is I wanted from that man. Remi obsessed over me. The very thought of me made his dick hard. Nothing pleased me more than to serve him and I made sure he felt it so why would he destroy what we built so easily and with someone who was of lesser caliber than I?

When I got home, my living room became a courtroom where I deliberated amongst a jury of my own mind, heart, and soul. my mind laid out the facts: Remi was caught in his office with another woman both fully exposed. Yet my heart examined the evidence: video proved that Remi maintained his innocence. My soul, however, had come to a verdict before either of them even begun to debate - I had to see Remi.

It had been a month since I'd seen him. Negative thoughts ran rampant through my mind like he had already rejected me before I got there. My heart seemed to crack and shatter more with every step toward my door. The doorknob was like a piece of ice that rested peacefully in an arctic ocean of guilt and sadness. Turning it felt like lifting a fifty-pound cinder block. I'd never prayed harder that the elevator would just so happen to get stuck, and it would be hours before maintenance could respond. I didn't want to go but I knew I had to.

A dark cloud loomed over his house as I arrived. The air around me was dismal. Remi was always good with keeping his yard maintained yet it looked as if no one had been home for weeks. The weeds grew wild, and the bushes flaunted stray branches bordering the path to the front door. It was a lullaby of pandemonium.

Remi never asked me for my copy of the key to his house back so when I pulled it out of my purse, my fingertips enjoying the familiarity. My hands quivered attempting to unlock the door. In trying to be quiet, everything became so loud. The birds in the neighboring trees all came over to perch themselves on the gutters above and began squawking instead of singing the sweet hymns they were singing on the other side of the fence. The winds rushed through the yard hard enough to bang on the windows. Even the key itself sounded like metal gears turning to start up a cruise ship when I inserted it into the slot. It was as if the nature around me betrayed me to alert him to my presence.

When I stepped foot into the foyer, it was almost pitch black. I let the light in, drawing back the curtains so that I could see. The house was empty and quiet. At least his housekeeper understood the assignment. I couldn't find a speck of dust anywhere. I toured through the main level, quietly looking around. There was no sign of him, but I felt he was close, so I called to him.

"Remi?" I beckoned, yet there was no answer. I navigated through the poorly lit corridor that led into the main living room. Even with the outside looking as if no one had been there all week, the entire first floor was exceptionally tidy. I thought to myself that if we worked things out, Christina was absolutely getting a raise. I looked around for signs of life where there were none. Attempting to creep up the stairs, I was then startled by a crash coming from the kitchen. I dashed over in a frenzy to discover Remi stumbling to the floor with a half empty bottle of corn liquor in his hand.

"Oh my God, Remi. What the hell," I muttered, throwing my purse on the table to catch him. He looked as if he had seen a ghost when he laid eyes on me.

"Mandisa?! Deesie…Maze…baby I'm so sorry. You left and didn't let me explain. I didn't fuck that girl. Baby, that bitch meant nothing. Nothing I swear!" he begged. He reeked of booze and body funk. His beard had grown tatty, and his waves turned into calm seas. He clung to me, snatching handfuls of my clothes to get his bearings straight but ended up dragging us both to the floor instead. His hands weren't the soft manicured ones I remembered that were now rubbing my face. They were hard, cold and in need of lotion. He continued to plead his case as he rested his head on my chest. My arms wrapped around him, holding him tight as I began to silently cry in contrition. He was reduced to shambles. What had I done to this man? Why was he in such dire straits in my absence?

"Baby, I'm so glad you're here. I missed you. What did you do to your hair? I love it!" he drunkenly exclaimed. He was child-like in his petitions, cleaving to my body and nestling his head in my neck. I attempted to encourage him to move.

"Remi, we have to get up. We can't stay on this cold floor."

"Huh? Oh, right right. Yea, I can get up," he slurred. He tripped over himself and failed in his struggles to help me up. When I was able to stand, he flung his arm around my shoulder and insisted he could make it up the stairs. Two steps forward, he stopped and looked as if he was focusing on not dying.

"Remi, come on. You ok? What's happening?" I asked.

"N…nothing. I'm.." *hiccup* "…I'm…" *hiccup* "…I…" he slurred, just before vomiting all over me. I was disgusted. I rolled my eyes hard enough to win some money. He apologized in excess. The chunks of what may have been green beans or cottage cheese, laid plastered all over my blouse. If I hadn't loved him and felt it was my fault for his decline, or had it gotten in my hair, I would have dropped him right where he thought he was standing. As he shuffled to the stairs, I stood next to him, soaked in vomit, and helped him upstairs.

"Maze, can we get in the shower? I stink..."

***

I stayed up all night in Remi's lounge chair crying. Fortunately, he hadn't gotten rid of my clothes, so I was able to shower and change after he launched his stomach fluids at me. I couldn't bring myself to lay in the bed with him because we still needed to hash things out, but I watched him like a hawk all night out of concern. The room was cold to keep him comfortable and to quell anymore accidents due to nausea, but I was freezing. I hugged my legs in the chair to keep warm. My face was swollen from the flood of tears that ran down it and breathing became a chore as my nose was congested. The headache that made a home in my temples, blinded me. All I wanted was for the aching to cease. Remi became unsettled as he began to wake up. I remained still so that I didn't startle him but called out to him so that he knew I was still there. Seeing him roll over and hug his pillow conveyed to me that it was alright for me to leave him for a second.

I went downstairs to make me a cup of coffee and settle in on the couch. My heart was still hurting from seeing my love in that state. It was a foreign sight as he was always so strong. I stared into the mug hoping it would reveal the answers I was looking for. The steam saturated my nostrils as I focused and meditated to relax more. About ten minutes had passed before I heard Remi's footsteps thumping down the stairs. We caught each other's eyes and had an entire conversation without opening our mouths. Reaching the final stair, he broke the piercing silence.

"I'm glad to see you're still here," he said. The shame in his voice was pronounced.

"I had to make sure you were ok."

"Thank you," he smiled. My eyes followed him all the way

161

to the couch where he sat next to me. Vulnerability and longing washed over me as my body begged him to just hug me. There was so much I wanted to say yet I was too flustered to even speak. We sat there in awkward silence, each wanting to make a move but too scared to follow through. I placed my coffee on the table and geared myself up to ask the questions that needed to be asked.

"Remi, what happened?"

"It's like I said, I was in my office…"

"Wha…no. What happened to where me leaving you affected you this way?" I asked, watching Remi turn frigid. He stared into the floor as resentment greeted his face like an old friend. It took him a second for him to answer me. I witnessed the wall I inadvertently built around him shake and crack. He fought hard to remain composed but as he started opening up, tears began to form in his eyes and spill over slowly, one by one.

"When I was a kid, I watched my mother be abused by my father. He used to lay hands on her mercilessly. The bruises he left were…were gruesome," he disclosed. Swallowing hard, he found the courage to continue.

"One day my mother had enough bloody noses, so she left and didn't take me with her. I remember my father being passed out from drinking too much and my mother came into my room, hugged me, said she was sorry and the next thing I heard was the front door close. Guess who became his punching bag after that?"

Listening to his story created a whirlwind of emotion spinning through me. My immediate reaction was to hug him tight and show my sympathy for him having to endure that. He pulled me in close and freed himself.

"That's why you leaving without hearing my side beat me down. I was watching the woman I loved most walk out on me when I did nothing wrong, all over again. That's why I was so bothered by all the welts that time and why I never really went too deep into putting my hands on you too violently. It was triggering. But for you, I put my trauma aside. In honesty, what we had has actually helped in coping with it"

I felt horrible. I didn't know that about him. In all the years we've known each other, he'd never spoken of his parents, and I never thought to ask. I was always a firm believer that if people wanted you to know a thing, they would tell you, so I never pressed him. But uncovering his truth opened my eyes. I apologized to him for missing the mark when I always bragged that we were so in sync. We rested in each other's arms in silence letting our souls reconnect. I missed him and our embrace solidified the fact that he and I were meant to be together.

Remi

Telling Maze my truth was painful, but I guess my exis-
tence needed purging. I knew she would never fully trust me had
I not cut my chest open and revealed the darkest parts of me. My
mother and I have since attempted to mend our relationship, but so
much damage was done that I just left it at the "we good" stage. I
didn't make much effort after that to build on top of it. We spoke
here and there but just to let each other know we were still alive.
As fucked up as that is, I just had a hard time forgiving my mother
for abandoning me. Sure, she was getting away from her abuser
and when I became an adult, I understood it and was even happy
for her but the other side to her freedom meant she left me, and
I became the abused. The child in me never got over it. Now my
father – you can forget about it. He could die and go to hell for all I
cared. Once I left for college, that was it for him. I never went back
home. Haven't spoken a word to him since. I never talked about
these things with Maze before because I thought I had worked out
my trauma through therapy so there was no need to. But when
she left, it all came crashing down on my chest like a Mack truck
into a brick wall. I didn't know it would be that painful. It was gut
wrenching to watch her leave. But I was glad to see her back in my
home.
    It was almost like I'd seen a ghost, watching her come to
my aide. I had lost my footing trying to get the last bottle of Ever-
clear out of my cabinet when I fell. Who the fuck put it so high in
the first place? I said I was going to fire my housekeeper, Christina
the second I sobered up because nobody asked her to do that. I was
just looking for something to keep the depression at bay. I clumsily
dragged Maze down with me as she caught me, and I began apologizing to her profusely. Desperation took the main stage in my
voice as I tried to plead my case. I wonder was this the little boy
reliving my past an enacting what I would have said or done had
my mother come back. Little me probably would have internalized
her leaving and felt like it was my fault. I would have clung to my
mother to keep her from leaving again just as I clung to Maze for
dear life.

It seemed like she didn't want to hear me though. I think she was more concerned with getting us both off the floor and into a more comfortable position so that I could sober up. Trying to get up must have been too much motion for me because as soon as we stood and stumbled our way to the staircase, my body started to run hot, and the onset of nausea started to kick in. She knew something was up as she paused and asked was I ok. I wasn't. I could feel the liquids in my stomach rising up to through my esophagus. Trying hard to hold it in, I tried to respond but ended up vomiting all over the poor woman. I don't remember anything after that until the next morning sitting on the couch next to her.

…But I was really glad to see her.

Mandisa

"What happened last night?" he asked. I scooted closer to him on the couch to warm up. He was still feverish but a lot more sober than the day prior.

"Well, you had a little too much hooch and threw up all over me. I had to clean you and me up."

"Yikes. Really? I'm sorry, baby. Dinner later?" he teased, popping his head up to look at me. His puppy dog eyes caused me to swoon inside, and I couldn't control my giggle. His proposition reminded me of when we first reconnected and I just couldn't help but bite my bottom lip in excitement.

"Sure. I'd love that actually,"

"Cool. Take the day and pamper yourself. Hair done; nails done – all that. Be back here by 6:30. You'll have a dress waiting for you," he instructed. His dominance came down and covered him like robe over a lost and found king. The authority in his demeanor consoled me. In honesty, while we were separated, I felt like a lunatic without her straitjacket. He kept me sane. Sure, I pretended to be ok like nothing was wrong, however, inside I was a mess. Remi had the power to save me from the world and in some instances, the world from me.

"What color would you like to see on my nails?" I asked. Like my panties, he always picked what colors he would enjoy seeing grip his dick. The selection shocked me this time. Usually, it was a combination of royal blue (his favorite), and an offset color. This time he wanted solid black.

I did as I was told and began my self care. The first stop was my hair stylist. She was able to squeeze me in last minute as I was only getting a simple style. I sat by the sinks and leaned back so she could wash my tresses. As her fingertips rubbed my scalp clean, the smell of the shampoo enticed my nose. I closed my eyes and thought of Remi. The idea that it was so easy to just come back to each other with simple apologies and warm embraces stirred up feelings of uncertainty. Was he going to kill me after dinner? He'd have plenty of places to hide my body. This was too effortless. What was he plotting at?

166

When my hair was done, my stylist turned my chair toward the mirror. I looked luscious. She brightened up the red which highlighted my skin tone so well. It hung long and wavy down the side. The bangs were the panache my style needed, and the layers were as even as two enemies calling a truce. Remi would be so pleased. I decided that my nails needed to be as fierce as my hair. While Remi chose the color, he always allowed me to choose the design. If the color was black, the offset had to be grandiose. I chose a coffin shape at about an inch long. The ring fingers were embellished with silver leaf and my middle fingers gave a huge 'fuck you' to the planet, fully adorned with crystals. The rest of my nails were black, as Remi requested. I felt like the baddest witch in town, ready to cast spells on the world.

As I returned to the house, it was still. Candles were lit from the stairwell leading up to the bedroom. As I found my way inside, there was a long black dress draping the foot of the bed. The satin was split with a lightning bolt of lace striking from the shoulder, wrapping itself around to the bottom. I whispered Remi's name in admiration with a smile bright enough to overpower the darkness of the room. I went to shower and get right for the night. I was excited to spend time with Remi even if it didn't result in us officially getting back together.

Wrapped in a towel, I wiped the fogged mirror to get a better look at myself. My hair was pinned up so my curls wouldn't wall from the steam. My thighs gently rubbed, and my ass poked out ever so slightly. My nipples were so hard, they had shown through the thick towel. My skin felt softer than usual that night. Water droplets waltzed down my bare neck and made a dancefloor of my chest. I was a bombshell pleading with the world to take shelter before I exploded.

I dried off and encased my body with a layer of sweet-smelling lotion before taking my hair down. I took notice to a black lace bra and thong set, resting peacefully next to the dress. I slipped the thong on and nestled it in between my firm ass cheeks. The bra sat the girls up higher than any other bra I owned. I stood once more in the bathroom mirror and put a hint of make up on. I kept my lips nude because my hair was so bright and gave the corners of my eyes wings.

The dress slipped on without resistance. It cuddled every curve of my body like it was the big spoon. Either Remi was secretly watching, or his timing was just that impeccable because just as I wondered how I was going to zip it up, he walked through the door. He smiled when he saw me and asked if I needed help. I smiled back and nodded, sweeping my hair to the side. I turned around so that he could admire me and complimented his choice of dress.

"I knew you would love it," he boasted. I bashfully smiled, turning to look at myself in the full-length mirror resting up against his wall. I did look god-like. The lace strip coming down the dress teased the eye with my skin. I could've bested Cinderella the way my shoes slipped on so easily. When my ensemble was complete, I turned to Remi with the anticipation of a grammar schoolgirl headed to her first day of class.

"Ready?" I asked, waving my arms out so he could get a good look at me. His eyes were locked on me as he stood back studying his own work of art.

"Not yet. You're missing something," he replied. My heart shattered and fell to my feet as he turned around and walked to his dresser. I turned around to the mirror, nervously looking over myself to see what was wrong with my look. I was flawless. What more could be added to my outfit that would make me more appealing. As I began to get discouraged, Remi slowly walked up behind me, kissing me on the side of my neck that was open.

"This is for you," he said, handing me a black velvet box. I looked back at him and then the box once more. As I opened it, my eyes lit up at a beautifully set tear drop ruby hanging on a platinum chain with diamonds surrounding it like a Queen's first line of defense. I was speechless.

"I was going to give these to you the night I asked you to come to the club," he clarified.

"These?" I inquired. Taking the box from me gently, he placed it on the dresser and opened another box.

"That one is for you to wear every day. This one...", taking a diamond encrusted collar out the box, clasping it around my neck, "...is for when I'm ready to fuck you mercilessly."

Every bit of air was snatched from my lungs as I stood there stunned. I ran my finger through the O-ring to make sure it was real. When it curled through it, I took one quick gasp of air and held it. I didn't know when I'd be able to breathe again after setting my eyes on what I've been begging for. Remi enjoyed the sight of me flabbergasted and kissed on my neck between instructions.

"This collar says I own you. As your Dominant, I vow to protect you with my life. I'll provide you with the love and care you need. There is nothing you will need or want for. Whatever you desire, I've got it. As my submissive, your only job is to walk in front of me like this world owes you money. Obey me, honor me, love me, Maze and I will worship the ground you walk on. Are we clear?"

We didn't make it to dinner that night. Our evening was spent creating an unforgettable space where we could be free to fully explore the rabbit hole I had so desperately been wanting to fall into. I was now a collared submissive. In my surrender to him, I became the most powerful person in the room. With every curl of my spine and scream that escaped from my core, I grew more uninhibited. I wanted him longer. Harder. Deeper. My freedom came in the form of my submission. I became a monster hungry for more with a Master who had no problem feeding me.

I guess this is where my villain story truly begins: in a king-sized bed, underneath a man I just pledged my entire soul to. Given the power to rule over a god by simply following his lead. A submissive able to bring the world bowing to her feet with just two little words:

"Yes, Daddy"

***